THE HUES OF SAMSARA

JANUSHI RAICHURA

ISBN 979-888503663-4

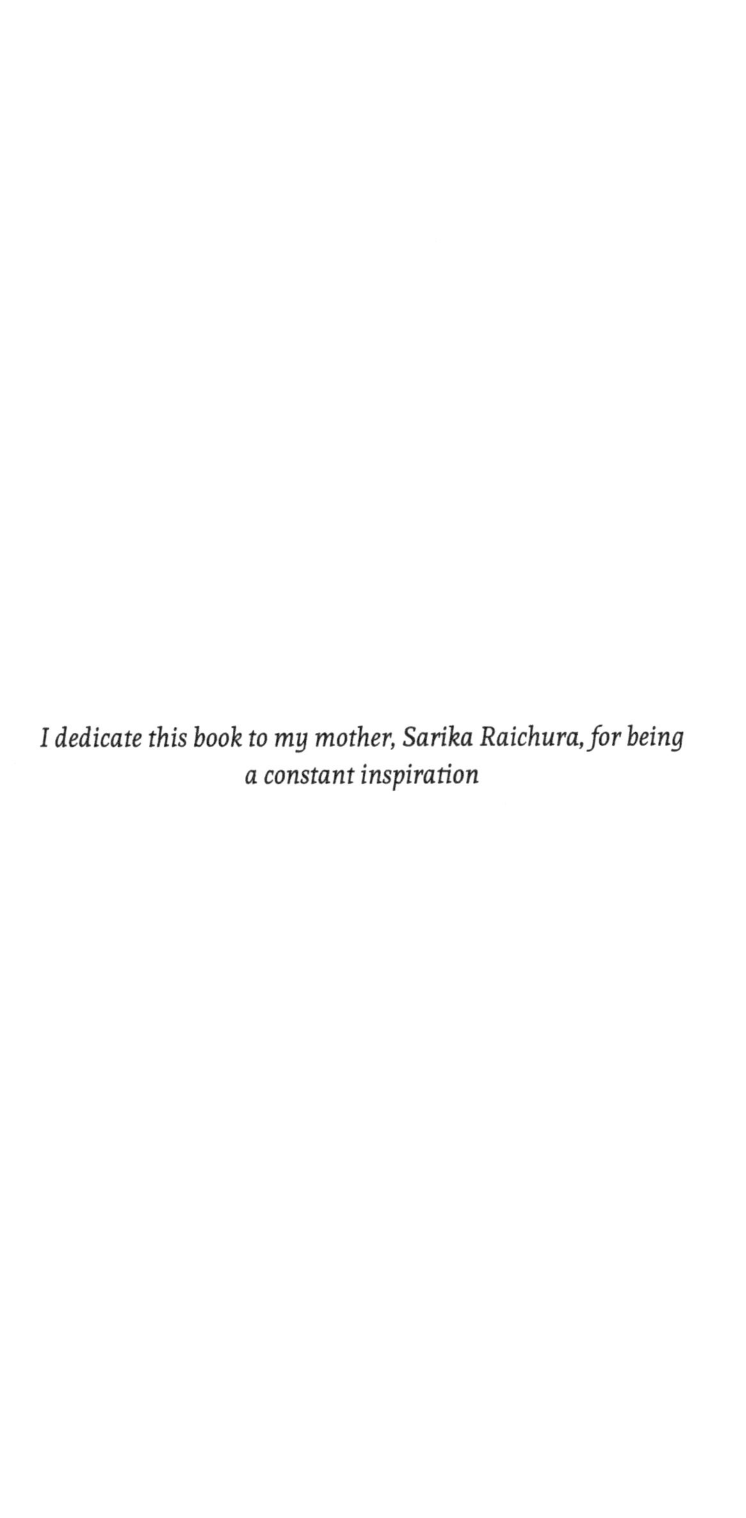

I dedicate this book to my mother, Sarika Raichura, for being a constant inspiration

Contents

Preface

I am more beautiful than any princess,
I am uglier than a crow,
I am more colourful than a rainbow,
I am colourless like a tear,
I am brighter than the sun,
I am darker than any night,
I am sweeter than any candy,
I am bitter than a bitter gourd,
Warmer than a hearth,
Colder than an ice.
I am kinder than anybody else,
Horrifying, I am death.

Most of would think why I have used good adjectives for death. You might think, death is so cruel, it separates loved ones. But does it? Now, I don't think I need to explain how death is bad, but I will explain you how good it actually is.

Death is beautiful as it takes the good people to a land, a place they deserve, heaven.

Imagine someone who is very good but has a very bad life. Death makes it colourful.

Death is bright, as it takes us to the light, the creator, the god.

Death is sweet, since it reunites the souls after death.

Death is warm, as it takes the soul away from this cold hard world.

Death is kind, as it frees the people, the soul of all its burdens.

It is my belief that in ways death is good. But we must not forget, in ways it is bad also. So, think of Death good and bad. Think of Death as something that is everything. Or maybe nothing. We have no memories of our preincarnation. Why? Death takes that away from us. If we see it clearly, Death takes everything away from us and Life gives everything to us, who we are, what we are, everything. Doesn't that make Death void? Or does it make Death devoid? We don't know.

But what we know, is that Death is something that is everything and nothing at the same time. Then why are we afraid of Death? What is it in Death that we are afraid of? Being away from a loved one? Maybe. Or being alone? Possible. But what we truly fear from Death is something known only by our soul. Only and only our soul knows that. But how do we find out? Every time we find out, Death takes away our memories. Why? Because it says that we should move on. We shouldn't be stuck somewhere. We should keep going. Even in Life, even in Death. We should forget about our past. And why be afraid of something that is eventually gonna come and there is no way to stop it. Why be afraid of it then? Why be afraid of it if we know that it will take us just to another Life. Death is like Night. Life is like Day. Every day we are given a new chance at our Life, and every Night, we know, if we have done a good use or a bad use of it. Every Life for our soul is a new day, a new chance. And every Death for our is Night. Where we know if we have succeeded or lost. So, I believe that you are afraid of Death, don't be. If you are afraid of going to hell or something, then be a good person and Death will be good. If you are afraid to be away from your loved ones, don't be. Remember, you will forget them after Death, the pain, the guilt, after Death it will all wash away. And if you are are afraid of pain and misery for them, remember, it is their Life of which you were a part of. They will face pain and sorrow and problems, but they will move on one day. And move on not in the sense, forget you, but in the sense, knowing that you are in a good place and they have to face life. If you are afraid of losing someone to Death, imagine the best Life for them, something you could never give them, they will have that in Death. So, don't be afraid of Death. Think of Death as another Life. Keep going, and think of Death as a reminder, that past is past, it cannot be changed, keep your arms open for future, and even if you don't know what will come in the future, know that it will be just another stage of this Life.

ONE

DEATH BED

My life was always different, even when I didn't know about it. But it supposedly changed after I had the worst headache of my life. And sometimes I wish the secrets were kept secret; for when revealed, they made everything a thousand times worse.

I exhaled, holding my head. I had the urge to bang my head against the wall, but I knew it would only make the pain worse. I was having crazy dreams, that lead to headache due to my best hobby; overthinking, and I had spent my whole afternoon searching for ways to deal with the headache. One thing about headaches: they are the worst. Had it been a stomachache or some type of body ache, I could just distract myself by watching TV or reading or studying or something. But with headache, it only made things worse; and it invited my worst demon: boredom to pounce at me. The pain was easier to deal with than boredom. Because when I am bored, I think, which causes more headache. I closed my eyes, trying to sleep but an image from my nightmare appeared. A little girl running on the roof of the apartments I lived in, and someone pushing her off, and she falling to death. I had this kind of dream before, when I was five. A baby thrown from the roof of a castle. I had an excellent memory when it came to dreams. Somehow, I remembered every detail; which surprised everyone but me.

I got up. I hated doing nothing. It was a waste of time, which I hated. I sat on my chair near my study table. My diary lay open in front of me. I grabbed a black marker from my pencil stand and started doodling on my arm. I drew two symbols: a crescent shaped moon behind the trapezium of my thumb, and a circle with a half circle and a plus symbol beneath it.

I had no idea where it came from, but I just felt the need to draw it. Over the years, I had learnt many things. Let me reframe it. Over the years, I have learnt everything possible. From drawing to singing to dancing to everything. Even some weird things like fencing and Latin and different symbols from different mythologies and looming.

The symbol felt familiar. I got up and took out another diary from my shelf: the one in which I note all the symbols I learn and their meanings. I flipped pages to the Alchemy section. It was filled with the symbols used by the Alchemists in the ancient times. I turned some pages until I saw the symbol. Beneath the symbol I had written: Pluto. For a careless moment, I thought it was nothing until, it hit me. It wasn't just the symbol of Pluto. It was also the symbol of death. Chills ran down my spine. I tried to convince myself it was a mere coincidence, but I couldn't. Because I knew, it wasn't. The reasons I studied different symbols was because I doodled them around; symbols whose meaning I knew not. And then I searched their meaning on the internet. Then, I started researching different symbols. I often had dreams about different symbols and languages. So, I started learning different languages too. I knew, three Indian, three Europe and an international language. I know how to write in Morse code and runes. And, I am thirteen. I am captain of two sports teams in my school and the class topper since kindergarten. I am what other mothers call, "Good example!"

I have friends, a lot of them. Best friends too. But I am a girl who loves shadows. That's where I stay. In the shadows. Apart from my achievements, people don't pay me much attention. Let me correct that sentence; Apart from my achievements, people didn't pay me much attention. But that was until I drew that symbol on my arm. Which changed everything, I stood for. I stood for someone who no one tangled with, because they knew better. I stood for the good quiet girl, no one paid much attention, I stood for revenge, the sweet taste of vengeance. For excellence. Now, I stand for forgiveness, for using silence as a voice not a way to hide in the shadows, for being noticed, for perfection, for precision, and above all, for being a hunter.

This is all present. I'll take you six months into the past. Back to the day, the moment, I drew that symbol; the symbol of the devourer, the end, the inevitable, or so I thought.

The symbol stood out on my pale white arm. And for once, I felt glad that I was having a headache, for I couldn't overthink about the symbol. At least not at that moment. I grabbed my purse and walked outside my room to my grandma's.

"Granny, can I go to the pharmacy? I couldn't find the medicine for my headache. I think I misplaced it somewhere."

"What's that symbol?" she questioned; worry lines deepening on her face.

"I just doodled it by mistake. It's nothing."

"It's not nothing. It's the symbol of death."

"How do you know that?"

"I have studied on that particular subject. But the 'how' is not important. The 'why' is important."

"I told you, I drew it by mistake. It was an involuntary action."

"You should be more careful. Drawing symbols like this: never ends well."

"What do you mean?"

"Go get the medicine you wanted. We'll talk later." I nodded, I knew better than to question her decision. I took the key of our house and close the door behind me as my grandma settled for her fifteen minutes evening beauty sleep. I walked below the early evening sky, sun blazing in front of my eyes. The pharmacy store was nearby. Right around the corner, as my dad said. I used my purse to block the sunlight and turned around the corner. As usual, a middle age man sat on the counter with a table lamp and few other medical stuff. The shop was covered with green wallpaper and the chemist was reading a newspaper. I had been there before twice, once with my grandma, and once with my brother Reyansh; but I had never noticed anything. At that time, I felt the urge to observe everything. The newspaper was of the previous day, I noted. Then mentally yelled at myself for that. I had bigger problems. Behind me, two men entered the shop. They looked like they were in their twenties and they were whispering something to each other. The chemist heard them and put down his newspaper. "How long have you been here? I am sorry if I didn't notice you."

"It's alright. I just got here."

"So, what do you want?"

"A little help. My head hurts, so I am sure what medicine I should take. I was thinking aspirin, but honestly, I am sure."

"I'll give you something mild." He said smiling. He rummaged around and came back with a box of tablets.

"Thank you." He removed his spectacles, and handed me the medicines. Reading lenses. I noted.

"Sir you want something?" he asked the men behind me. They turned to face him, their face mixed with anger and confusion.

"Excuse me?" one of them asked.

"He's asking if you want any help."

"No, we're fine." The other one replied, his eyebrows raised.

"Um...okay," I paid the chemist who was staring at me, in wonder and confusion.

"What's your name?" the first man asked.

"Grandma says not tell strangers my name."

"But we're not strangers, are we?" his accent turned thick and I realized something. That was the first time we talked in English. We weren't talking in Hindi before. Or Gujarati. We were talking in foreign languages. European. Spanish, French and Latin. In that perfect order.

"Do I know you?" I asked in English, trying to calm myself.

"It's a nice tattoo. I can sense death around you."

"I have to go." I spoke bluntly and ran outside the store. The strangers didn't follow. I unlocked my house as fast as I could and entered. I closed the door behind me. "Grandma! Grandma!" I called. No reply. I rushed to her room. She was sleeping peacefully on her bed. A little too peacefully. Death symbol. Negative thoughts rushed into my brain. I shook her. She didn't move. I pushed my thoughts aside and called her name several times. She didn't answer. I called my father, who was at work.

"Dad, it's nanny. She's not moving."

"Calm down, tell me more precisely, what happened?"

"Nanny was taking her nap and now she's not waking up!"

"Call the ambulance, I'll get there." I took out my nanny's phone and called the ambulance. A lady picked up the phone. I told her it was an emergency and told her my address. She told me the ambulance will arrive within half an hour, so i sat down to wait. By the time the ambulance came, i tried moving my nanny, but she didn't move. I had called my brother Reyansh who arrived just in time for the ambulance to come. They took my nanny's pulse, which i could've checked, but I was too afraid. Afraid to face the reality. My mom had died when i was young, so nanny took care of me; and now I didn't know if I could handle it if she died too.

TWO

HUNTER'S HEARING

My brother took my hand to comfort me while they checked her pulse. They told me something I already knew; there was no pulse. No breathing. They checked if she was really dead or just brain dead. But she really was dead. Gone forever. I controlled tears that were threatening to fall off, I didn't wish to cry. I could just think of one thing; if she died because I drew that symbol. It seemed impossible. But the coincidence was too much to take. My brother called my dad and from the expression on his face, I could tell he was barely holding himself together. We called some other relatives of ours. My grandma's sister, was the first to arrive. She was a lot like grandma, the same cheery self, but right now, even she was grim. We did the rituals. My nanny's body was to be burnt the other day, by which all our relatives had arrived. Everyone was crying hysterically. Everyone but me. I managed to stop my tears until they moved the body, when my control over my tears broke, and I wept on my aunt Krishna's shoulder, who held me. Everyone but my maternal aunt Krishna, maternal uncle

Kedar, and my aunt Krishna's son, Vihaan, who was my brother Reyansh's age, left. I haven't told you much about my brother. He was every definition of cool. He cared a lot for me, loved me a lot. He wanted to be an interior designer, so, he had a designer's head, so our whole house was designed by him and me.

My cousin, was a typical brother. He wasn't cool, but protective. It was like he was my real brother. He was close my brother's age, around twenty-three. We often went to national parks and science exhibitions together. He was studying medical and he had his exams coming over in a month or so; but still he had agreed to spend the night with us. That was the thing I liked the most about him, he put family above all. We put up an extra bed for him in me and my brother's room. At around eight, we had dinner, which was cooked by our relatives at their place. They brought it over to our place and we all ate together. It wasn't much. Just normal *sabji, roti* and rice. During dinner, everyone tried to make small talk, but with a dead body in your house, believe me, it wasn't easy. My aunts looked at me and my brother with pity and my aunt Krishna, even talked to me in private, saying that if I our needed a mother, she would always be there. My aunt Krishna is nice. Very much like my mother, as people say, but I would never know, since my mom died when I was five.

It was just another normal day, I had woken up in the morning from the night I mentioned before, about a baby thrown from a castle's roof, and I started crying. My dad woke up and soothed me, my mom didn't. She never woke up. In the morning, dad tried waking her up but it was useless. I was too young, so I didn't understand what was happening, my brother Reyansh did. He took me to another room and told me that mom had gone for a long sleep like bears did every winter. And that she would wake up and come back by the end of the winter. But she didn't. I spent my day with my cousin brother, Vihaan, at his place. Everyone acted normal around me, but even the five-year-old me knew everything wasn't normal. Something was wrong, I told my brother Vihaan my nightmare that day. He looked at me worried and told me not to worry. I still remember his eyes widening with apprehensiveness when I asked him if my nightmare had something to do with my mom going into a deep slumber. He didn't reply, he just hugged me and said that everything would be fine. That winter, I stayed with my aunt Krishna and her husband, my uncle Abhra for a while with my brother. Then for a while with my uncle Kedar and his wife Tulsi. They all treated me like their daughter, but I missed my mom. Because mom is mom, she's irreplaceable. My nanny's death was like a replay of my mother's death. I sat with my brothers, Reyansh and Vihaan. We sat in silence for a while before I spoke.

"Something happened today." They both glanced over in concern.

"What happened?" my brother Reyansh asked me worriedly.

"I went to the chemist for a headache medicine-"

"You went alone? I have told you not to go alone outside the house!" brother Reyansh interrupted.

"Let her complete!"

"Thanks brother Vihaan. I met two men, who talked to me in Spanish, French and Latin and I didn't realize that until they talked to me in English. And then they told me they smelled death around me and that we weren't strangers. But I had never seen them before in my life. And then I came home, more like ran home and I found nanny dead. And a little time before I left, I subconsciously drew the symbol of death on my hand. What's happening, brothers?" tears rolled down my cheek and brother Reyansh put an arm around me to sooth me.

"Nothing's happening to you. Just get some sleep. You are overthinking." I nodded. Brother Reyansh and Vihaan exchanged glances and I could see a silent agreement going on between them. They were hiding something, I knew it, but I was too tired to care. I turned off the lights and pulled up the sheets and went to sleep.

I woke up at around midnight, to the sound of approaching footsteps. I could tell there were two people, and from the sound of the footsteps, they were both adults. I heard the main door of the house close and I could hear both the people enter.

"Today there were two, tomorrow there would be dozens."

"Nani's soul covers her. She is safe."

"For now. We need to call Amara. She is the only person who can protect her!"

"Have you lost your mind? Amara? You know every time Amara gets involved, she dies. He follows her. Wherever Amara goes, he follows. He'll kill her like the last five times."

"Kill who?" I asked standing upright, when the footsteps stopped inside my room. In the faint moonlight, I could see both my brothers Reyansh and Vihaan at my door.

"We were talking about a video game, Sarika. Just go back to sleep." Brother Vihaan told me softly.

"A video game? Since when do you play a video game?" I asked sleepily. "And what were you doing out of the house at this hour of night."

"We went downstairs to feed a dog." Brother Reyansh answered, hesitantly.

"You went downstairs to feed a dog, at three in the morning? At least make some convincible excuse." I yawned and pressed my head back into the pillow. "I am going back to sleep."

They walked out to the veranda and due to my dizziness, I could vaguely hear them speaking to each other.

"Don't call Amara. She's danger. He'll follow her and he'll kill *her*." He said the other her as if he wasn't talking about Amara.

"Look, she's our only chance. And she would've learnt from her mistakes, right? I mean you think the sixth time she would be a little more careful?"

"There has to be another way. She's safe for now. We still have a couple years-"

"Shush...."

"What?"

"Her hunter skills. She can hear us." Brother Vihaan reduced his voice so much, I could barely make out that line.

"Look, I told my friend to set a trap for the enemy when it enters. Now, let's get back to sleep. We'll play it after they burn nanny's body." Brother Reyansh spoke in normal voice. I was so tired, that I couldn't quite understand what as going on, and before I knew, I was asleep again.

THREE

Control Over Life

Death is inevitable. We have no control over it. But what about our life? How do we control it? *Do* we control it. How much control do we have over our life? I believe, the answer is zero per cent. We have zero control over life. The more we try to bring it in control, the more it goes out control. Humans have tried to control nature. But the thing is, life, like nature, doesn't like to be controlled. The more we try to control it the more it goes out of control. What happens when we try to control a tornado? Can we control it? No. Nature is the only thing that can control nature. Just like that, life and nature are the only things that control thing that can control life. The life of someone else controls over life. Our fate. Some stranger might have made a big change in your life and you might not have known it. Something funny done by someone else, makes us laugh. Makes our life enjoyable. The only we have control over, is our mind and body. How we control our mind against things and how we take care of our body.

Some people want control over everybody's life. Imagine being in control of everyone's lives. Imagine having control over everything. Decisions are hard to make. Imagine being have to make decisions over everybody's lives. And imagine the responsibility coming with it. Imagine the pressure. People losing their money, lives, because of your decisions. It could drive you insane. It could drive anyone insane. Therefore, you have no control over your life, the only thing you have control over, is your own self. Your self-growth, your health, your hobbies. Life goes on. It always will, you can't stop it. You can't control it. What you can do, is keep up with it. Go on with it. The more you try to bring it in control, the more it will go out of control.

So, it is just better if we have control over just two things. Two very important things. Our mind. And our body. And leave the rest to fate and hope for the best.

FOUR

Weighing Losses

Dear diary,

Death. It scares me, for it is quite terrifying. Life is depicted as a journey with a destination. But I don't think life is as simple as that. I believe, life is story, a story with no end. I don't believe death is the end. My culture believes in reincarnation. So, if our sould goes on, how is death an end? Souls are immortal, indestructible and eternal, so hoe death an end to something that has no end? I believe death is just a phase in the eternal life of the soul. And I wonder, why we fear death. Why I fear death. I wonder how my mother is. Has she had another reincarnation or is she with the god, I wonder.

I can't take the loss of my grandma. I loved her. She was the closest thing I ever had to a mother. I don't know, why she died. I don't know why god took her away. I tell myself everything happens for a reason, but what could be the reason for her death. And I wonder what my brothers meant when they said that nanny's soul covers me? Was it my fault she died? I drew that symbol and maybe that's what caused her death. Or maybe I am overthinking. But I can't stop thinking. I can't stop blaming myself. Today, they burned her. I stayed back with my aunts while the men in the family went to the cemetery. I cried real bad and caused everyone else to cry more than they already were. They say she's still around me, with me and somehow I can feel her presence. But I don't see her. And I badly want to. She wanted to tell me something, but because of my stupid headache, I will never find out what she wanted me to know.

Sarika

I didn't usually wrote in a diary; I only wrote whewn I really needed to talk to someone, and I had no one. My brothers were hiding something from me. They wouldn't seriously be talking about video games when our grandma had died. They faced grief and moreover had decency.

All the men went to the cemetery, while the women stayed back. For a while, everyone stayed quiet. Then they started having small talk. I sat alone in my room and cried to myself. Now and then, someone would come in the room for something and would see me crying and start crying themselves; which made me feel like everyone would've been happier if I hadn't been there. At last, my aunt Krishna entered the room to see me. She was crying and I could here commotion behind her which indicated the men had returned from burning my nanny's birthday.

"They're back. You shouldn't sit here alone. I'll send Vihaan and Reyansh to keep you company. And talk to them, they're your brothers." I nodded. "And I'll tell them to close the door behind them."

"Whatever you say, aunty." She left and few minutes later, my brothers entered. "She's really gone, isn't she? She never gonna come back." I asked.

"We need to talk." Brother Reyansh said.

"Go ahead."

"Your school starts back tomorrow. You need to go there, you need to get our mind off things. We have told your class teacher what has happened. She has said that the teachers will lay off you for a while. And it's fine if you haven't done your weekend's homework."

"I did it on Friday evening. It was about family background. Nanny helped me with it." Brother Reyansh sighed and sat beside me along with brother Vihaan. He put an arm around me and I started sobbing. He gently patted my back while brother Vihaan poured me a glass of water from the jar of water on my beside table. I took the glass from him and sipped down the whole glass.

"So, who's Amara?"

"Who's who?" Brother Vihaan asked blankly.

"Amara. That girl you were thinking of calling when you went down to feed the dogs at three in the morning."

"Feed dogs-at three? Sarika, are you okay?" Brother Vihaan asked worriedly.

"Really? Now you're gonna pretend that didn't happen?"

"Sarika, you should really rest. You cried yourself sleep last night; you must've had a dream."

"It wasn't a dream. I asked you who was Amara and you said you were talking about a video game."

"Do you seriously think we would be talking about video games on the night of our grandmother's death?" I shook my head. "See, right there you got your answer!" I was confused. There were chances it could be a dream, but I believed what I say, and I believed my brothers were lying. But I couldn't just say that. The logic was on their side.

"I am sorry. It's just I am so tired of everything. Of people dying, and I just want them to stop dying. Especially on me."

"I know." Brother Reyansh spoke softly. "And I am sorry you have to go through all of this." We sat together in silence until lunch. My aunt Tulsi came in to call us for lunch. I was neither too close nor too distant with her. We were neutral. We talked when either she came over or when I went to her place. Mostly, I talked with Aunt Krishna. Aunt Tulsi was nice too. It was just that, I had known aunt Krishna my whole life, aunt Tulsi just got married with my uncle Kedar a few years ago.

"You boys, go and have lunch while I talk to your sister." She said putting up a smile. Her voice was honey sweet, an so were her words. She radiated warmth. And talking to her could relax anyone. Brothers Vihaan and Reyansh left and aunt Tulsi came to sit beside me.

"Look, honey. I know we aren't very close. But I want you to know, that you can always come and talk to me like you talk to your aunt Krishna. And know that your both brothers will always do what is good for you. Trust them to make some choices for you."

"What are you talking about?" I asked blankly.

"One day, soon, you'll know. Now, come on, let's have lunch."

My uncle Kedar and aunt Tulsi had a daughter. So, Aunt Tulsi went back to her home for the night, while my uncle Kedar, aunt Krishna and my cousin Vihaan had to stay back for thirteen days since they stayed the first night. My aunt Krishna's husband, uncle Sagar had gotten brother Vihaan's books for him and I and brother Reyansh were under strict orders from father to not disturb him. I went to school from the following Monday. Not everyone knew about my grandmother, just my close friends who I had texted from my laptop and my teachers. I sat on my place allotted by my class teacher. It was right in front of my best friend, Aheli, besides my competitor, Achal. Like I said before, I am the topper. Achal ranks up right after me, in second place. Most of the time, I score more than him. Sometimes, we tie. And very rarely, he scores more than me. We had a test today. A small one. Of 10 marks. But I knew I had to score more than Achal. I suddenly had a desire of winning; one I had never had before. It was a math test, so Achal had an advantage; most of the time, we tied in math test, and that was when I had studied hours before the test. Today, I had no chances of winning. Our first period was math and our teacher handed us our test papers. Achal completed before me and gave me a smug smile before handing the teacher his paper. I finished two minutes after him and then came back and started reading my history textbook. We were starting a new chapter in history today, and I hadn't studied over the weekend; so I had to at least read the chapter. After everyone finished their papers, ma'am gave us some sums and started checking our papers. We got our test results by the end of the class. Achal got his paper first. He had got a 9.5, and his face fell as soon as he read the numbers. He shot me a look of jealousy and put his paper inside his bag. Then I got mine. And I got my lowest marks ever in a 10 mark test. 8.75. Those numbers were easy to make him grin.

"Aw, little girl need a tissue?" he asked slyly. I faced him, my face lightening up again. I went to my teacher and showed her the miscalculation. She had miscalculated and given me 8.75 instead of 9.75. I got back and resisted my urge to shove my paper in his face. I simply put it on my desk and he gave me a murderous look. The day went well. My history reading came handy when teacher asked general questions and I answered them all correctly. Suddenly I had the need to be in the spotlight. The teachers had thought that I would just stay quiet like I always do when something like this happens, but this time I didn't hide. I showed everyone I was the topper. There was no use of being one and just showing it in exams. The teachers liked me for my silence, so when everyone failed to answer,

I volunteered, unlike the times when I knew but stayed quiet. Some teachers looked worried by this, while some appreciated it. By lunch time, I was already called by our class teacher to 'talk' and believe me, she seemed really worried. I don't know why, though. Isn't it good, I put myself out there? For me, it is. And I am starting to enjoy the attention I get.

After going home, I first completed my homework and went to the park. I live in a township, everything's here. Chemist, super market, park, even a school, the school I go to. Most of my friends stayed here too and so do some of my teachers. So, I have always had to be appropriate while going around here. I had brought a book to read and I sat on an empty park bench and started reading it. I read for around an hour and was stopped wen a softball hit me on my head. I turned to face a group of really young boys playing softball.

"Sorry," one of them yelled apologetically.

"it's alright, sweetheart." I said throwing the ball back at them. A lady, who looked around my brothers' age, appeared next to me.

FIVE

Forever Is Too Long

"Is this place taken?"

"No. Do you wanna join me?" I asked smiling. She nodded and sat beside me. She didn't look very happy, she seemed of a sadistic nature to me. She looked quiet, not shy, exactly, but it seemed as though she was lost. She wasn't Indian, I could tell. But she didn't look foreign either. She had brown hair, that came just below her shoulder. She had side bangs on right and her clothes were really decent.

"You're mourning someone. Who is it that you lost?"

"Someone really close."

"I feel your pain, having faced it, not once but on several occasions."

"Did someone you love die recently?"

"Not recently, yet it seems like yesterday."

"Who was it?"

"My mother, she was murdered."

"Oh my god, how?"

"We were just a normal family, me, my mom and my dad. My mother, she had something a lot of bad people wanted. But she and dad were really powerful. And the only person with the ability beat her, was my dad. My mom, she was strong, quick, agile, powerful, kind, and most of all, she trusted dad with her life. She didn't see it coming. One night, after dinner, dad cuffed her. I was in the next room, I heard my mom scream and I ran there, where my dad looked at me with those cold eyes, I had never seen them. He forced me to go into my room and locked me in there. I heard them go outside, more like, I heard my dad force her outside. I got out through room's window and I saw torches lite in the distance. Torches like not the electronic ones, the fire ones. I quietly got there, without making any noise. My mom was tied there and there were two man, and a lady along with my father. She didn't give them what they wanted, so they killed her. And my father just stood there and when I screamed, he walked up to me casually, like nothing had happened, and threatened me. I ran away. Since then, we have met on very few occasions, and none of them have turned out to be good."

"I am so sorry. I understand the loss of mother. Mine died too when I as five." My words shook her. She seemed to have forgotten I was there.

"I am sorry-I shouldn't have blabbered like that. We don't even know each other." She apologised hurriedly and picked up her pack, standing up to leave.

"Wait. What's your name?" she regarded me for a moment before replying.

"Amara," she quickly turned and left while I stood dumbfounded as the realisation hit me.

ᑭᑭᑭ

Dear Diary,

Forever, is a long-long time. Why do we die? That's an easy question. To maintain a balance. Now imagine, we have everything. A never-ending space for humans, never ending resources, everything. Even then, Death would be necessary.

We often say the word forever like, "I could listen this song forever" or "I could eat this for my whole life"

Now imagine you can't die. Would you really listen to that song forever? Would you really eat that food item forever? No. You'd get bored.

That's the thing about humans. We get bored in like a snap. When you live forever, time means nothing. I mean it. Everything that used to mean, doesn't mean anything. Love, hatred. We just get bored of them.

Why do we need to die? Because we humans have a tendency of getting bored of something really easily. We often say, "I'd would love you for my whole life,"

But if your life is never ending, wouldn't you get bored? I mean you wouldn't admit it, but how long would you love someone, be with someone until you get bored. In movies, yeah, two lovers never get bored of each other. But in reality, we could either bond and develop an intimacy or get bored.

Option two has a higher possibility if you think about it. Say you love one person forever. What about the others? You would get bored. You know, if we were vampires, maybe we wouldn't get bored, but fortunately, we are humans and the god has blessed us with love. A love that even Death cannot take away.

I don't know why I wrote that, but as I sat on the terrace of my house, the words just put themselves there. I put my diary aside and starred at the sky. Everything was dark. Our building was the highest in the whole township and we lived on the top floor. Mom liked this one because she said it helped keep an eye on things, and I agreed. I could see everything from there. And the quietest whispers echoed up to the terrace so I could listen to the conversations of anyone in my house. I closed my eyes and focused. I could hear an argument going on right under me.

"You called her here?"

"I didn't call her."

"Then who did?"

"I don't know. I just saw her at the part with Sarika."

"What was she doing with Sarika?"

"She didn't know who she was until she blabbered everything to her."

"She told her everything?"

"Not everything, just the modified story. Look, Amara will help us. She is the only one who stands a chance against him."

"He'll follow Amara."

"We are all doing everything we can to keep him away."

"You can't keep him away. He is too powerful."

"We have the power of the three gods, the tridevas on our side. He cannot defeat the gods." I slowly opened my eyes. I felt bad eavesdropping on my brothers' conversation, but somewhere in me, I knew I had to, and that it was about me. I picked up my diary and pen and got up. I patted my jeans to shake off the dust and stole one last glance at the moon before turning and leaving. On my climb down the stairs, I tried putting the pieces together about Amara and some killer.

I knew for sure I had met Amara at the park, and from what I had just heard, I knew she wasn't telling me the whole story. And that she told me something I wasn't supposed to know. I thought about what it could be, but couldn't think of anything. Someone was following Amara who would kill some other person, who, mostly was me. But like I had read somewhere, a murder requires a motive; now I couldn't think of one reason why someone would want to kill me. I was just a normal thirteen year old girl. Normal didn't seem right, maybe I was unique, but still, why would someone want to kill me. What had I done before, that had gotten me to point of someone planning my murder.

Then some random words hit me.

We have the tridevas on our side...the symbol of death...I can sense death around you...Pluto...nanny's soul covers her...

And then*Amara* toppled it all.

Pluto was not only the symbol of 'death', it was also the symbol of 'rebirth'. Amara meant immortal. Suddenly I remembered something, a flash. I remember the number eight on Amara's neck which was concealed by a scarf. Eight, horizontally, is the symbol of infinity. And the way she talked, it felt as though her parents weren't just politically or capitally powerful, they were physically strong too. And who could be stronger than an immortal being?

Amara was immortal, I knew that now. So was her mother, but somehow, she died. And her dad wanted the secret of immortality, so he killed her. And maybe Amara knew the secret of immortality, so she was being followed too. Now, I didn't think her dad followed her, because immortality cannot be just cast out, it could be transferred to some other being. So, most likely, when her mother died, her immortality was transferred to her dad. And the three bad people. Maybe one of them was following Amara to know the secret of immortality and the rest were either dead or lived in fear of Amara. As I entered my apartment, I ran over to my desk and noted it all down so I don't forget it. I made a quick mind map and hid the book in the middle of my other diaries just in time for my brothers to enter.

SIX

TIME

The most powerful of all. One that bows to none. One that rules overall. Ever wondered why time never stops running? It never stops running so that no one ever catches it. It just keeps on going. Always stays ahead of all. No one has ever won from time. It has crumbled down everything. Every great ruler has bowed to time. Even the gods respect time. Time can be the greatest healer or the greatest destroyer; for it is the master of all. The worst thing is that even time cannot control time. Time cannot speed itself or slow itself. It cannot stop itself from being the destructor. But we must remember, the destructor, is also the builder. Time builds relations, hobbies, emotions. Everything is built from Time. It is the start and end of all.

Time is the best inspiration we can have. Like Time, we should make our presence important. So important, that everything is meaningless without us. To be the master of all. To be the builder, but the destroyer, too when threatened to outrun. All the living beings bow to Time. Time teaches us to be the best. To be impossible to be outrun. To be better than yourself.

For ages, scientists have tried to have control over it. But Time is a puzzle that even time cannot solve.

This is a quote written by my elder sister, Janki Raichura,

"Be like time, Jack of none, Master of All"

SEVEN

HIDE OR DIE

"We need to talk," brother Reyansh said firmly. I nodded towards the bed on which all three of us sat down together.

"We know you met Amara," brother Vihaan started. "And we know that you have heard most of our conversations. And we know you were just doing an analysis of what we just said." I looked at brother Reyansh but he just looked away.

"I am sorry...I just couldn't help but listen."

"We're not mad at you," brother Reyansh spoke glumly.

"No? Because it looks like you are."

"We're not mad Sarika, we're just disappointed." Brother Vihaan said.

"That's even worse," I muttered. All my life, I had never liked disappointing someone. Once I remember, I had lost a competition my dad wanted me to win. And he said he wasn't mad, he was disappointed and I had cried for over an hour. I was sensitive that way. I liked when people were proud of me, not disappointed in me.

"We expected better..." brother Vihaan stated.

"Well, what did you expect me to do, cover my ears?"

"No, we expected you to not talk to a stranger." Brother Reyansh continued.

"And I expected *you* to not lie to me. Not to my face at least. That was hurting. My both loving brothers, hiding things from me...lying to me! Wouldn't that hurt you?"

"We're sorry, okay? But Sarika, you must know, everything that we did, was for you. To protect you. But it seems you are well past protection."

"What do you mean?"

"What he means, is that no sacrifice can protect you any longer. You have to come out and declare yourself. Because the longer we try to hide you, the higher are the chances of you dying."

"What do you mean?"

"Amara will tell you everything, till then, you have to lay low. You see a stranger approaching or staring at you, you get out of there as soon as possible." I nodded. Brother Vihaan took a textbook of his and started reading it. He seemed upset about everything, upset from me. Brother Reyansh left the room and I sat down beside brother Vihaan.

"I am sorry, brother. I really am. I was just lonely and upset. And Amara seemed the kind of person who would understand me. And she just wanted to sit there. I thought it would be rude to say no."

"I have to study, Sarika, so let me."

"Brother-" I started but he cut me in middle.

"Let-me-study." He spoke aggressively. I backed away in fear. He rarely got angry and when he did, it never turned out pretty.

I put a hand on his and softly spoke, "Brother, please. I am-" I started but he roughly jerked my hand away and growled.

"Go away!" he shouted. I caught my breath. He seemed really angry. His pupils widened, and so did his eyes. He bared his teeth and I backed away in fear. He seemed to have lost control of himself.

"Vihaan!" his mother's voice brought him out of his aggressive state. He jerked his head sideways and blinked a few times. He took his head in hand and gulped. "You okay, son?" Aunt Krishna asked apprehensively.

"Yes, mom. I am sorry." He apologised to me.

"it's okay." I replied shaking. It felt as though he had turned into some other kind of person for a moment.

"Sarika, we have some news." My Aunt started.

"In a month or so, your dad, you and Reyansh are going abroad to get your mind off things. We would've come along, but you see, your brother Vihaan has exams coming up and we thought it would be nice if you all bonded together."

"I don't wanna go anywhere!"

"Honey, it's safest for you to be away from here. To be somewhere else for a while."

"Where are we going?"

"You're gonna like. You are going to Europe."

"We are going to my favourite place after my favourite person's death? Why?"

"Well, we thought going to someplace you like might lighten you up."

"I am sorry...but I wanna stay."

"I didn't wish to say this, but you have no other choice."

"Wow-just wow." I didn't wish to be dramatic, but I felt so heartbroken and angry that I just started crying.

"Sarika, stop being dramatic!" brother Vihaan snapped. I was hurt. I wasn't given a choice or wish. I was plainly ordered to just go somewhere.

"Dramatic..." I murmured and got up and left my room. I went up back to the terrace with my diary. I didn't write in it, I just wanted some privacy. About an hour later, my brother Reyansh came up to call me for dinner. I wasn't hungry, or sleepy. I just wanted to be alone, so I told him, I would come later.

Later that night, I was *informed* by my dad that he had booked the flight tickets, hotel, everything. I guessed that no level of drama would help me out of this. I and brother Vihaan didn't speak for days. As a matter of fact, I didn't talk to anyone more than necessary. Aunt Krishna tried to talk to me but I just politely avoided her. She, uncle, and brother Vihaan left after thirteen days were finished, and I know it's wrong to feel that way, but I was relieved. I cried myself to sleep most nights after that. No one noticed, they just thought it was the dizziness of morning. My brother started going to college again, and I returned from school before him, so I was alone for a few hours, and to be honest, I started feeling a little lonely after a couple days passed that way. When you are used to someone being around for long intervals, after their death you feel a kind of emptiness in your chest, that no tears, nor time could heal. Sure, you could fill it with someone else's presence, but it never leaves you the same. School was the same for me, except I had started getting some more attention. I had detached myself a little from my friends, and they understood why, so they didn't complain. I wasn't curious anymore about Amara or anything. The sorrow had overcome my curiosity. Sometimes I would have reactions when I was alone; like I would suddenly out of blue start throwing things around and cry. I would clear up the mess after calming myself down, and would never throw fragile things, even in my worst mood, because I had no intention of drawing attention to myself. I slept peacefully, with no or very quiet and normal dreams. And sleep was the only thing I enjoyed, and as soon as I woke up, I would wait for everything to be over and go to sleep. It went on for a whole month. Then, I was forced by my brother and father to go shopping for new clothes. And during that, I needed to have a full conversation with them. My mother's side of the family was filled with strict followers of God Krishna, and my father's side of family was filled with followers of Brahma. We were respected the most among the other followers of Brahma and Krishna. Our family name was widespread and well-known, as well as well-reputed, so I wasn't allowed to wear anything showy like shorts or a short crop top or off-shoulder. So, I just bought some different types of tank-tops, spaghettis, overcoats for spaghettis, and jeans.

"You got everything you like?" my father asked me as we exited the shop.

"Nope," I replied flatly. I could tell he was barely holding back his anger but so was I.

"Sarika-" my brother started.

"He taught me to be honest and truthful. This is just me being honest and truthful." He didn't argue. I always knew how to turn people quiet. We walked ahead not talking when I saw the photo of a dress on a in the shop we were in.

Recreation of Queen Victoria's most popular dress

It read. Below there was a really beautiful boat neck dress. Before I could admire the beauty of the dress, I felt a searing pain in my head. I fell on my knees holding my head.

"Sarika!" my brother said in surprise and knelt by my size, patting my back. "What's wrong?"

"I don't know," I answered and yelled as the pain increased the moment I started thinking about what was wrong and then I blacked out. It was the first time I had fainted. Oh boy, how much did I not wish for it to be the last.

I woke up in a hospital. Apparently I had blacked out for the rest of the day, because I could see the night sky outside the window of my ward. I could see my dad sleeping on the chair near my bed. I tried to remain quiet, but after a while I got bored. So, I thought to wake my dad.

"Sarika, how are you?" he asked sleepily.

"Healthy as a horse."

"No jokes." He said firmly, his dizziness fading.

"Whatever you say, father. I am fine. My head hurts bad. I am bored. And tired. Can we go home?"

"You have been advised to stay here for a night. We'll head home tomorrow." I made a face at that. "Don't worry, I'll be here the whole night."

I didn't want to stay at the hospital for the whole night. There was an extra bed where my dad slept that night. I was having trouble sleeping but was really tired, so I closed my eyes and stayed still, trying to quiet my mind to bring sleep. After what felt like an hour of being still like this, I heard footsteps. Someone from the outside tried to open the door of my ward. A part of me, thought it was a dream so commanded my body to be still, and not attract any attention. The person outside pushed the door open, breaking the lock, and confirming the incident being a dream. I could feel the person coming close to me.

EIGHT

MY LIFE'S NOT A JOKE

"It's a pity, actually, killing you. But I have to, even though I don't want to. It's for the best. I am so sorry, Sarika, as they call you. But I promise, that this will not be the end. I will find a way to end them, but till then, for her safety, I am sorry, I have to do this." Said the person in a whisper. I could tell he was a men and his voice seemed strangely familiar. It was assuring, counselling and comforting.

"For whose safety?" I asked in a whisper. If it was a dream, he couldn't hurt me. I might as well get some answers in the dream. I didn't open my eyes, but I could tell the man was surprised. He thought I was asleep. He didn't reply. I heard descending footsteps and he left. When I opened my eyes, it was morning. My dad was up and he was talking loudly on the phone with someone. Brother Vihaan was there sitting on a chair near my hospital bed.

"You okay?" he asked softly. I pretended I didn't hear him. Even though I wanted to know what was wrong, I wasn't going to talk to him. I was still angry at him. Like I was angry at everybody else.

"Sarika, are you okay?" my dad asked worriedly as soon as he put his phone down.

"Better than yesterday." I replied forcing a smile. I couldn't ignore him, it would just make him more anxious. "What's wrong?" I asked, trying to make conversation.

"Someone broke into our ward last night when we were asleep. We checked the CCTV footage He was standing near you. And then you muttered something, and we think he thought you were awake so he ran away."

"Really?"

"Yes. There was no audio, but it was pretty clear he wasn't there by mistake." So maybe, what I had heard the previous night wasn't really a dream. But the question was that why would someone wish to kill me? Sure, there were I lot of things I didn't understand. But I knew one thing for sure, I had done bad to none. Then why were bad things happening to me? Brother Vihaan stayed with me for a while, during which I went into the bathroom and changed out of the hospital clothes into my normal ones.

"I am sorry," Brother Vihaan muttered. I ignored him and walked away but he stood in my way. "That person, who came here last night; we don't think he was just a thief. What did he say, Sarika?"

"He said he wanted to kill me." I spoke nonchalantly. He froze and gulped. "You're right, he was more than a thief. He was a murderer."

"You think this is all a joke?"

"Yeah, to be honest, that is exactly what I think." I snapped. "You guys have been treating *my life* as a joke. I have no idea what is going on, yet you expect me to do everything you say without questioning. I lost my mother at the age of five. What part of you is so insensitive that you do not understand my feelings? I take it as a joke because

I don't know how I'll react if I believe it. All my life, I have asked myself one question, is it my fault that so many people around me are dying? And now I get the answer, that yes, it is all my fault. The fault of my existence. Had I not existence, everyone would be alive! Have you ever thought how I felt about all of this? Have you ever asked me, what I felt? So pardon me the, "Be serious, Sarika" talk. Because if I become serious, I won't be able to live with myself." I walked around him outside the door and found my dad talking to a doctor at the end of the corridor. I took a deep breathe and walked toward them. I meant what I said. I had done everything I could to keep my mind off the fact that all these deaths were because of me. I did everything in my power to not think about it, but all my efforts went in vain because of what my brother spoke.

I didn't blame him, no. I blamed myself. For everything. I wished I was more normal. Every part of me, wished to be normal at that point. To not belong to some royal religious family. To not be the centre of attention. To have a full living family. To not have to worry about being murdered by someone. To not have to be concerned about someone else dying at every moment.

Since I was young, I have always been sadistic. Dwelling in sorrow. I have never had someone I could rely on; myself. And I could only talk to one person; myself. I have always been afraid of being judged, so I never told anyone anything. I kept everything to myself. I avoided telling everything to my friends, not sure if they'd keep it all a secret. To be honest, half of the things I wrote in my journal were twisted truth. I was always afraid what if someone would read it. So, even after setting up so much security for my journal, I couldn't write all I wished to write in it.

My dad called me and I snapped out of my thoughts. He put an arm around me and asked, "Feeling better?"

"I am good," I lied. He looked at me with concern. "I am okay, father. Can we just go home?" Home. I had used the word a lot of times, but I didn't know what it meant to me anymore. Home is a place of comfort and familiarity. But even after living in my home for over seven or eight years, when I went home that day, it seemed so unfamiliar. Every home has a smell, a smell that eases your tension, calms your anger, I no longer felt that. The scent seemed to have vanished. I knew every inch of my house, yet that day, it felt so unfamiliar.

I was told to rest for day so I went to sleep as soon as we came home. Even though I had had a very sound sleep the previous night, I was still very sleepy. I closed my eyes and my mind drifted quickly to sleep. I had a very beautiful dream, but somehow, I felt sad, like I missed something...or someone.

I was running in woods. Pines trees surrounding me. I was faster, and I felt confident. I knew I was running after someone or something. I felt strength, I had never felt before. My speed was doubled, or maybe tripled. I felt light, agile. Even though the ground was rocky, I didn't hesitate or trip once. I saw the being I was hunting, and I targeted it. And slowly, I shot. It flew wild through the air and went straight through its heart. I knew that, because I heard the heartbeat of the being stop. "Well that was easy," I stated kneeling beside the dead being.

"I would use the word unnecessary. You could've caught it ages ago." I heard an oddly familiar and comforting voice.

"You know I love hunting. I enjoy the hunt. The fear they radiate. They deserve to spend their last moments in fear, afraid of death. It's nothing more than what they've given their victims." I replied, and my voice felt different. It felt mature, and peaceful, ancient, powerful and kind. Neither of which I was at that time. I felt a hand on my head, a hand filled with love and care, and the voice spoke,

"It's going to be okay. *You* are going to be okay. *We* are going to be okay." Even though I didn't know what was meant by that, I felt comforted and relieved and I woke up quietly. I could still sense that hand on my head, like someone had literally put their hand on my head while I was asleep. I heard people whispering outside my room and just like I did that day on terrace, I closed my eyes, and focused.

NINE

SHADOWS

Think of the sun as future. Something that must be faced. One that puts your past, your shadows, behind you.

To relinquish on facing the future, is to retrace the past; to let the past become your present or future.

When we face the sun, the future, the shadow, the past, remain behind us. But when we deny facing the future, it remains ahead of us.

We can't break our connections to the past, past will always be our shadow. What we can do, is not let it become our future. Sure, we can't erase our past, it will always affect future; but at least it won't be future.

TEN

SECRETS

"Dad, we can't take her there." I quickly recognised the owner of the voice. It was my brother Reyansh.

"We have to, son. It will distract and we'll be on move for the whole trip."

"What about her? You saw what happened to her today and that was just one gown. She collapsed at the sight of one gown, you know what will happen if you just take her to Europe."

"We have no choice. Amara's here. And he'll be here soon if he isn't here already. He wants Sarika dead. And he will have that at any cost. The only thing we can do is delay him, till she's ready."

"She's too young. She shouldn't be going through all this."

"She was born for this purpose, which she will serve. We can either pity her, or fight with her. We have to wait, till she is old enough to understand everything." With my eyes closed, and my head throbbing, I fell asleep before the conversation ended. I slept through the night. When I woke up, it was early morning. I was wrapped in two blankets, while I had fallen asleep with only one blanket on me. I realised I was still cold, so I rolled up like a ball and waited for a few minutes till I was warm enough to stand up and check the precise time.

I was still drowsy, so when I tried to get up, I got tangled up in the blankets and fell on the floor. Lucky for me, the blankets took the blow, but it was still very embarrassing. I checked the surroundings to see if someone saw my fall or not, but my brother was asleep, and apparently so was my father. I yawned and stretched a little before I went to get a closer look at the clock. It was five thirty in the morning, but I wasn't sleepy anymore, which I had it coming, since I had been asleep for over fifteen hours. The monsoon wind sent chills down my back so I took a jacket, put it on and walked outside the room to the veranda. I liked the wind brushing my hair, so I just stood there for a while, inhaling the humid fresh air. The son peeped from the horizon as the time passed. Just as the sun had enlightened the sky, and the weather had gotten a little warmer, it started drizzling. I took the clothes that were drying outside in the house and put them in a pile on the couch. I put my jacket along with those clothes and walked back out, enjoying the morning while I should've been getting ready for my school. Just as the clock struck six, my father's alarm went off, and I heard footsteps approaching me.

"'Morning, Dad." I greeted quietly.

"What are you doing up? You should be asleep."

"I have been sleeping for fifteen hours, not to mention the hours I spent resting at the hospital, I am good now."

"You sure, honey?"

"Yes, dad. Now, I'll go bath."

"You wish to go to school today?"

"Yes, I do."

"Fine then. Get dressed. I'll cook the lunch."

"Dad, do you need help in the kitchen?"

"I have been cooking for years now. I'll manage dear." I turned to leave after giving him a warm smile. Ever since mom's death, he had taken the whole management of the house. He used to manage his business, and look after the house. Nani dropped in from time to time to help him, but he was actually under a lot of pressure. And the thing that made him my hero, was that he never let it show. No matter how bad the day had been at his work, he would never take out his anger on either me or my brother. He would put us to bed every night, without fail, he would tuck us in, confiscate all the electronic gadgets from both of us and give me a good night kiss on my forehead.

Now as I grew up, I felt obliged to take some burden from him. Mom's dad had been as bad for him as it had been for me, but he was always the strong person. He loved her, and no one had thought that my mom, the most cheerful person to ever live, would die from heart attack at such a young age. It came as a surprise to everyone.

I freshened up, got into my school uniform, combed my hair and went outside my room for breakfast. My brother was still asleep so I avoided making noise. I had short hair, so combing them was very easy. I kept them open most of the time. When I was young, my brother would oil them and comb them for me. But I learned with time.

My brother was always so mature. He was the cool brother, but he was very sweet and kind to me. We rarely fought and when we did, we wouldn't stay mad at each other for very long. Our dad always told us one thing, "that when push comes to shove, the only people you would be able to rely on, would be each other. So, be as close and good to each other as you can. People give false hope, false signs of support, but they never mean it. You two are connected by soul."

And I believed him. I know he was right. Friends fall apart, cause no matter how much emotional bond they have with each other, they aren't related by blood. But when you are connected by blood, you just treat other like your responsibilities. And you don't run from responsibilities because of the guilt it causes.

By the time I was ready, so was the lunch. I always wondered how dad cooked so fast. I mean, I had cooked with him a lot of times for fun, but at those times we would work at my pace, which wasn't the fastest. I don't know why, but now I didn't wish for family time anymore. I wanted to be alone, left with my thoughts, in peace. They were hiding something from me, and I hated secrets. I liked everyone being open about their thoughts and activities. I felt like I was insane. Stupid. I opened my diary and started writing.

Dear Diary,

Deep down, everyone has a secret. Something they hide. Something from their past that they have told no one. For one reason or the other, it is always important, that the secret stays buried. I want to know my family's secret; I wish to discover it. I know it has been hidden for the better but I really wanna know about it, and I am past self-control. I need a plan, a plan to find out all that lays hidden from me.

Sarika

I thought for a while with my eyes closed. I didn't realize but I involuntarily drifted to sleep.

I saw three people in front of me and they radiated a very powerful aura. And it took me a while to realize that they were the three gods themselves.

"Do you promise to keep this a secret and use your gifts only for the greater good?" The god in the centre asked in a booming voice.

“I promise,” I replied, my voice unfamiliar, and very thick with confidence. The three gods raised their hands and started chanting in a different, ancient language. It took me a while to realize that they were chanting in different languages and voices. I could not see their faces since they were clouded by light. It came to my mind that maybe there weren’t just three gods there. Maybe different gods from different religions were there. Three most powerful from each one. I felt a surge of power. My skin glowed and I somehow knew what was happening. I had became the Immortal Huntress.

I woke up gasping. My skin felt like it was on fire. I was on my table, my head on my diary and my pen still in my hand. I blinked to clear my head. I was in my room, not in front of some gods. I was still a normal thirteen-year-old girl, and not an immortal huntress. The dream seemed funny now. Ridiculous. I shook my head and smiled to myself, closing my diary. Surprisingly, I had slept through the whole afternoon, and I felt fresh. So I decided to go for an early evening walk. I called my dad to take permission, but surprisingly he told me to strictly stay in the house. I put the phone down a little rudely and without saying bye, with just a simple blunt, cold ‘okay’.

ELEVEN

My Experiences With Death

I didn't care if he was being a protective father or not. If he was just being worried or not. I was safe. And I was old enough now to at least walk to a park that was twenty metres away. But of course, he had to be worried. Cause I was a two year old baby, who was not included in any family secret or conversation and had no say in where I was taken. I fell back on my bed, tears spilling out of my eyes for the lack of freedom. I wanted to be given at least some freedom. I agreed to whatever they said, but there was a limit to everything. I took the keys to the house and walked outside the main door, slamming it shut behind me. Enough was enough. I walked to the park and sat on the swings; thoughts jumbled in my head. I tried to focus on the ants crawling around me, or the birds swinging on the branches. But it was hard to forget that I had just disobeyed my father. There weren't many people in the sight, but I didn't care about that at all.

A young lady met my eyes. She was standing in a position that suggested that she was about to run and was just waiting for the signal. I saw another person, a man, at the front of a building. He was standing in a suspicious position too. I got up, realizing something was really wrong. I started walking calmly towards my apartment. The man followed and the woman-growled? Yes, she growled.

I could hear her run towards me, but before she could reach me, the man, who was at twice the distance at me, came between us, as I turned.

"How about you pick at someone your size?" The voice was very familiar. And I realized that it was the same voice I heard that night at the hospital. But I had heard it before too, I just didn't remember when.

"Get out of my way!"

"Not a chance." He put a hand on her shoulder and her body started withering. She aged a hundred years in a matter of ten seconds and collapsed on the ground. He turned to me with a smile.

"What was that?" I asked, shaken up.

"Nothing, my luv," he put a hand on my cheek and my mind was pulled into darkness. "Just a bad dream." I heard his faint fading voice.

I wasn't sure if I was awake or not, if it was a dream or not. I felt like I was standing on the brick of darkness. And that I would fall in it any moment. He took me in his arms like I was made of paper, but very carefully, like I was as easily breakable as glass. Just as he started walking, I heard a sharp voice from behind him. And I immediately recognised the owner of the voice, Amara.

"Where do you think you are taking her?" she asked.

"Does it matter, darling?" he asked back coming to a pause.

"Put her back in her room," her voice was commanding.

"You must be joking."

“I am not. This doesn’t have to turn uglier.”

“Amara, let us both agree that I am stronger than you. And I will very happily, hurt you if it comes to that. So, I think it’s safer if you just get out of my way.”

“Where are you taking her?”

“Taking her would be a too polite phrase. I am just going to throw her off a building or something.” I involuntarily snuggled up close to him in his arms.

“I can’t let you do that,”

“Can’t let me? Seriously? Girl, who do you think you are?"

"The Immortal Huntress’s daughter. And a warrior like her. So, I am not going to let you take her. Even if it means I will have to fight you.”

“You know what? All this drama is making me sick. I’ll just put her in her room and kill her some other day.”

“Why do you never just simple twist her neck or stab her?”

“I am not cruel, Amara. Power-hungry, yes, but cruel, no. I mean how can you actually let an infant die in your own hands. Throwing her off is always easier. At least that way I don’t have to see her in pain nor do I have to look deep into those eyes reflecting betrayal.”

“Well, at least that shows you are still human.”

“Honey, don’t expect more from me. You’ll just end up breaking yourself carrying the wrong impression of me.” I felt a gust of wind brush my hair and my mind dissolved in the darkness as the cold wind lulled me to sleep.

I woke up on my bed, tucked in properly and wrapped under two blankets, but realized I was still cold. I got up and saw that my brother was sitting at his desk, studying.

“What time is it?” I muttered sleepily.

“Oh, glad you’re up. I was starting to get worried. It’s seven, by the way.”

"What! It was just four a minute ago. And then I went downstairs and there was a lady. And there was a man. And then there was another lady named Amara."

"When I came up here, you were lying across the bed, like all across it. It was so unlike you. I thought to peacefully put you to sleep. It must have been a bad dream."

"It felt so real." I whispered; fright clear in my voice.

"Hey, it's okay." Brother Reyansh said soothingly. Getting up from his chair, he put a hand on my cheek. "It must have been a really bad dream. You are burning up. How about some more rest? I will wake you up for dinner."

"Sounds like a good idea." He kissed me on forehead. I closed my eyes and peaceful sleep easily found me. Gladly, I had a dreamless sleep. Which I was very much thankful for. I felt nausea surge through me as I got up and off the bed. It was dark, and my brother was not in the room. My feet felt like jelly, like really, I could not feel my bones. I held a chair for support and then relied on the wall to get to the door. I slowly opened it and bright lights instantly went into my eyes. I moaned. Apparently, my brother and father were taking out some suitcases at that time, and both were taken by surprise by my sudden arrival.

"You're up," Brother Reyansh noted. "You hungry?"

"Very," I replied, my stomach burning with hunger.

"Come on, Sarika. The dinner's on the table." I clumsily followed him to the dining room. I felt feverish and I knew I had a cold, cause I could feel something in my throat. I made my way to the dinning table.

Days passed faster than I could imagine. Before I knew, I had gone to Europe and had been back. Originally, our trip was of three weeks, but cause of me, we had to cut it short. No, I didn't throw any tantrum, I can assure that, it was just that, every time I would see a monument or something kind of ancient, I would have a bad migraine. I blacked out five times, in three days. For all those who find it funny, I just have one comment, "MEAN!"

We got back after spending four days there. But neither my brother, or my father looked disappointed about the fact that our trip was ruined. As a matter of fact, they didn't mind it at all. Not even one bit. We had spent one day at Athens, Greece. We saw the Parthenon, my favourite monument. Though, I could've watched it better. If I wasn't too busy collapsing on a rough rock. Then I saw a statue while returning from the hospital. Guess what? I ended back at the hospital. Hilarious. We then went to Rome, Italy, the other day, on an aircraft and got there in about an hour. We spent an hour at the Colosseum. Luckily, I got an hour to admire its architecture before I fainted. Twice that day, actually. Once at the Colosseum, and once at the hotel at the sight of a painting. Then the next day, we went to Turkey, where we visited the Temple of Artemis. And you will not believe what happened? I made it through the whole time there without collapsing. And just when I thought things were looking up for the better, we walked out of the temple, and I fainted. Again.

Then my dad just booked a ticket back to India. In short, it was the best trip of my whole life. Sarcasm intended. Life was so much easier when I was younger. Here, I was at a hospital for a week. And there were a lot of needles involved. My poor skin. The doctors said I lacked nutrition. Brother Vihaan talked with them, and well, the only words I could understand were, 'IVs' and 'nutrition', though they were enough to warn me about what was to come. I wasn't afraid of needles, but they always gave me a kind of déjà vu feeling. Like knives did.

TWELVE

TRUSTING THE DEVIL

"Coming after me? What do you mean? That day you thought you were dreaming, you weren't. At hospital, you were tried to kill. And before that at the Chemist's store, those men would've killed you, had it not been for your brothers. You see, the three bad people, Amun, Zakara, and Baif, they found a way to link the body of others to theirs. They have their own personal army."

"Oh, great. So are you telling me, that I was having flashes in Europe cause I had seen it all as Sara."

"You got that right."

"Good thing I didn't go to the Temple of Artemis as Sara."

"You did go there. See, Artemis is also an Immortal Huntress, so being around a place with her power, gave you power, it cleared your head." I mentally thanked goddess Artemis.

"Can I ask you something, Amara?" she nodded so I went on. "You are the most powerful of them all. Yet you run. I wonder why."

"You taught me to hunt, mother, instead I became the hunted. It's funny isn't it? Everyone ran from you, I run from everyone. You know, you taught me one thing, 'Either you are at the top of the chain or you're in it. There's no way around.' I am in it, right now, and you were always at the top. You and dad. If I was stronger, I could've fought dad, I could've helped you. But I was weak! I wasn't strong enough."

"You were not weak, Amara. No one weak can bear so much."

"Don't try to make me feel better,"

"I don't make people feel better, I just state the truth, Amara." She stared indistinctly in the evening sky. I hadn't noticed how beautiful the view was outside. The monsoon sky had turned a unique blend of blue and grey. As if on cue, it started raining heavily. "Why are you telling me all this now?"

"To offer you a choice. You can either choose to fight them right now, against all those who were responsible for your death, or-" she took out a necklace from her jacket's pocket. "You can wear this. It will block your essence and aura. They won't be able to find you. You will stop having those headaches too. And no one else will have to die. The choice is yours. You can have a normal life at least till you are thirty. And then, when you'll be more mature, when you would've lived a life, you will have to face them."

"So I have choose between the life of an heroine or a boring girl. You know, I always wanted to be normal. A quiet little girl. It seems stupid, since I no longer have a chance at a normal life. But I want to give it a try. I am done dealing with deaths, sorrow, pain. I choose the necklace." Amara handed it me and the moment it was around my neck, she vanished. Why leave like a normal human, when you can leave like an immortal huntress?

A few days went by peacefully. Things were starting to get back to normal which was honestly, a relief. But it was hard to forget about all the drama. I had missed a lot during my trip and when I was in hospital and on bed rest, so I spent most of the time catching up, which distracted me, but I night, before going to sleep, I couldn't think of anything but the wonder what would've happened if I had chosen to fight.

One evening, I was walking around close to the park because I was very bored. But I was so wound up in thoughts that I bumped into someone. It was a man.

"Pardon me," he said but he didn't continue walking. Suddenly, I felt very much aware of the fact that there was no one around us. I looked at his face, and I had never seen someone more handsome. He was tall, his skin was fair, and he shared Amara's eyes.

"And had godly looks." I remembered what Amara had said. And I knew who I had bumped into.

"I know who you are. I heard you talking to Amara that day. She doesn't like you much. And something tells me you are not very likable."

"Sweet. I need to tell Amara to stop making me look like the bad guy."

"Well, you can't blame her. You are a bad guy. I've heard about you. You are the reason her mother died, aren't you?"

"You know, you're right. And now, you're gonna come with me."

"Why would I do that?"

"Because, if you don't, I am gonna kill you." He stated simply.

"I can take you," I said with fake confidence.

"Yeah...I don't think so. You see, I am the most powerful hunter in the whole world. And the only person who could take me is dead. So, don't be stupid."

"And I was that person who take you."

"You were immortal back then. And trained. Come on, you can't compare yourself to me. Now, come with me." He lead me to a outdoor coffee shop.

"You know my brothers will find me."

"And if you don't shut up, I'll kill them." That shut me well. He told me to sit on a chair in front of him on a small white circular table. "What do you want to eat?" I just pointed at coffee on the menu. "I asked what you wanted to eat, not drink. Never mind...waiter!" he called and a waiter appeared. "Get us two cups of coffee and a cheese sandwich and a vegetable sandwich. Now, you listen to what I have to say." I nodded, fear building up in my chest. "Good. So, I listened to what you told Amara the first time you met. And I want to tell you, that you couldn't be more wrong. Her father didn't get her mother killed for her. He got her mother killed for himself. For his self-growth. For his own selfish reasons. And I would know, because I am her father." I winced, getting more scared by the moment. "Yes, yes, yes. I know this might come as a surprise. But I can't believe you are so stupid. I know you were stupid enough to marry me in your preincarnation. To trust me. But I never knew you were so stupid to not accept something that happened right in front of your eyes." He sighed. The waiter bought two cups of coffee and two sandwiches. "Eat," he said gliding the cheese sandwich towards me. "I know you like it. And I know you're hungry." I didn't have much say in the matter since I had to stay shut. I just nodded and took the plate and started eating slowly. I could feel my hands shake and tears at the verge of falling. "Now, now. Don't cry. You'll create a scene." He said tucking my hair behind my ear. My phone rang in my pocket. "Give me that." I gave my phone to him. "Ooh, it's your brother. It can't get more interesting." He answered the phone. "Hello, Reyansh. She is right in front of me, sipping coffee. Your sister's a hunter. I am sure you have some of her skills. Hunt her down." He cut the phone and put it back on the table.

"Please don't hurt my brother." I pleaded.

"I'll think about it."

"I am not stupid." I said quietly.

"Uh-huh. What makes you say that?"

"You would never hurt Amara."

"Go on."

"She's your daughter. And I know that you loved me. And I can't think of one reason except your love for Amara to get me killed."

"I'll give you one. Your power."

"How's that a reason? We were equally powerful. It wasn't as though I was more powerful. We were equals."

"That's the thing. Men don't like to be equal to a woman. They like to be above them."

"I don't think you believe that."

"Now, why would you say that?"

"Because we are on the same table, eating nearly the same things."

"But you're afraid me. I am not afraid of you. That doesn't make us equals."

"I am not afraid of you."

"Well, you should be. You know, I could still kill your brother when he gets here."

"You won't kill him."

"You think I am bluffing. Is the goal that you hope to accomplish worth your brother's life."

“Tell me, how does it feel to be feared by your own daughter?”

“Shut up...” he said coolly picking up a butter knife and twirling it between his fingers. He was threatening me, but I didn’t care. He was going to kill me either way. This was my best shot.

“To threaten her?”

“Okay, your last warning to shut up.”

“To know that she would’ve cried for years because of you. To kill her mother in front of her.”

“Seal your lips.” He said putting the knife under my neck.

“To hear her begging you to not kill her mother. And yet doing it and hearing her scream your name in agony.” I could feel the blade dig my skin.

“Hey!” I heard someone yell. We both turned to the sound of the voice. It was my brother. Stanford threw the knife to the ground.

“Get your sister out of here and I might let her live.” I could see rage flicker in his eyes. And my confidence melted. He back away from me and brother Reyansh took me home. I took one last glance at him to confirm what I had seen. I knew what he was doing. He was trying to make himself look like the bad guy. So that Amara would hate him. Because it would be easier for her to bear the fact that Sara died because of him than to bear the fact that Sara died to protect her life. So that the villains would think that he was bad and would tell him everything he had to know to keep his daughter alive. I had got what I needed. To be sure that he wasn’t the bad guy.

THIRTEEN

TOO MANY SCARS IN A STORY

I was very dramatic at first. I would shout and yell and throw tantrums. Be very childish. But slowly, when I realized that they were gonna do it anyway, I just gave in. Let's just say those two weeks, weren't the best weeks of my life. Finally, I was discharged from hospital but I was told to have bed rest for at least a week. Slowly, as a few days passed, things started getting back to normal. I started missing Nani a little less.

Dear Diary,

Time heals all the wounds, but the scars are enough to remind us of the pain.

Medicines are healers. They heal wounds. But what about the mark left by them? The mark left by the wounds? They go away, eventually. At least from the outside. But what about the inside? Scars sometimes disappear. Sometimes we disappear before they do. But as long as we have them, it'd belike we have a photograph of a moment. The difference is that the moment is bad in this case. But don't think of scars as a mark of pain. But I think of them as a mark of survival. The mark of something

I have survived. Survival is hard, but it sustains me. Ever scar has its own story. But the story of scars doesn't end there. It is a mark of survival that hides pain behind it. Just because a wound has healed, it doesn't mean it's gone. It leaves a mark on both our body and mind. And unless it has gone from both of these places, it isn't truly gone. It is there, like a sign with something buried inside. Something whose trueness is only known by the bearer of the scar.

Sarika

I put the diary away, when I heard a knock on the door of my room. I turned around to see my brother, who entered my room, and was shortly followed by a young lady.

Amara.

I recognised her as soon as she entered. She had a grim smile on her face. And she sat on the bed alongside my brother. "Sarika, may I formally introduce you to Lady Amara."

"Hi." I waved shyly.

"Hi, m-Sarika." She also spoke shyly and hesitantly.

"Amara here, is going to tell you a story. I'll give you both some space." He politely excused himself and left the room.

"Over five hundred years ago, was born a girl named Sara. She was loved by all, but she was not like the other girls. She disliked being treated like a damsel, and her father, taught her the art of shooting, hunting, to put it more precisely. She excelled at it. Never missed a prey, but as she grew older, her mother started getting worried about her marriage. And so, she was banned from touching the bow and arrow. That was it. Sara run away, deep into the woods. She had a kind of fierceness in her eyes that only warriors had. She was quick, smart, strong, and she was impeccable at the art of survival.

"One day, she came across an archery competition being held at a kingdom. She heard that the prince was undefeatable, and that all who thought they could defeat him at archery, were welcome to try. She took it as a personal challenge. When all men were defeated by the prince, she challenged him."

"Let me guess she won?"

"No. It was tie. And before the final round, the king ordered the soldiers to capture her."

"Why?"

"They thought she was a witch. No, wait, that doesn't seem right. They didn't like the fact that a woman had been regarded as the prince's equal. So, well, they arrested her and made everyone believe that she was a witch. She was to be burned at a stake at the dawn. They had tied her up in iron chains. Priests used salt and chanted outside her cell, to trap her. Later that night, she heard footsteps outside her cell.

"Psst.." a voice whispered.

"Who is there?" she called.

"Prince Stanford. We competed this morning."

"Is it dawn already?"

"I don't like the fact that you are being killed like this. It's wrong."

"I don't need your pity."

"I am here to free you." The cell's door opened, and Sara was greeted by the handsome face of the prince.

"Thank you, Your Majesty."

"Run. Go East. The soldiers will steer clear of you. And if you get surrounded, fake a spell. They think you are a witch; they will be scared." Sara thanked the prince and ran down the tower outside the castle. She knew how to hide, how to be quiet. She started protesting against the biasedness, ruthlessness, cruelness. She started rebelling, fighting, silently killing all the monsters in human form. And then, finally, she moved to the kingdom of Prince Stanford. There was a carnival going on, and the king had given his presence. She hid in the woods and aimed right at the kings heart. She believed that those who bore no heart in spiritual sense, deserved none in the physical one. She was about to shoot, when someone grabbed her and pressed her against a tree trunk.

"What do you think you are doing, lady?" Prince Stanford.

"The right thing,"

"Is that what you think you are doing? This is revenge."

"It's not revenge, it's justice. The gods would've stopped me if I was doing something wrong."

"The gods haven't stopped him. Does that mean he's done no wrong?" Sara looked away. "You want revenge, huh? Kidnap me."

"What? Why? You have nothing wrong!"

"There is one thing."

"What have you done, Your Majesty?"

"There must be something. Or you wouldn't have stolen my heart." Sara was confused, she couldn't decipher the meaning behind those words. "I am just joking, m'lady. I need to ask something from you. I no longer wish to stay here. Can I run away, with you?"

"Why me?"

"Cause you are the best huntress I have ever seen. And you owe me a favour."

"On one condition. Help me those monsters." They ran all around the Europe seeking justice. They were in the Viking region, when they got married. And suddenly, one day, Sara and Stanford were offered immortality by gods.

But the gods had one condition, that they keep fighting off the bad guys with their immortal powers. They were more powerful than normal humans. Lighter in weight, and so, faster. Had an amazing sight. And had godly looks. These gifts were offered by all gods of all the mythologies. These gifts were there, cause their soul and body were linked. And so, they were as beautiful and powerful as their souls. As light, and clear-sighted like their souls. They accepted the gifts, but asked for one thing in return, that if they ever have a child, he/she, would be made immortal too. The day they turned into immortals, they created a weapon to kill them, in case something led to that situation in the future. Centuries went by in peace. And they had a daughter-"

"Named Amara?" I asked.

"Yes. When she was mature enough, she was turned into an immortal too. But she wasn't like her parents. She was very bad at shooting or any sport. She was a pretty pink princess. She could cook, sing, do gardening, knit, but no, she couldn't hunt. Sara and Stanford weren't disappointed, cause they loved her. But she always felt like a disappointment. She didn't want immortality, but she felt like that was the only thing she could do for her parents. The three of them posed as Lord and Lady around the world. They did have a lot of gold from the people they had killed. And there was something about them, that made everyone respect them.

"During the World War-2, they came to India. They were here, helping us Indians against the British. But the Europeans had heard of their immortal existence. And they convinced Stanford to turn against Sara. The Europeans wanted the secret behind immortality. So they could create Immortal Soldiers for the war. I have already told you the rest of the story."

"So, you are immortal, right?"

"Yes. Two Lords and one Lady became immortal cause they managed to break the link between Sara's body and soul and then linked themselves with their souls. And now the main thing. Sara's soul reincarnates again and again. And she is the only one who can kill them. She and me. So, every time mom, Sara, reincarnates, I go there for her protection. They follow me and kill her. That's why I am alive. Cause I am not strong, I am weak. And think I am incapable of killing them. They have the weapon to kill me, but they use me to their advantage."

"No offence but, why are you telling me this story?"

"Cause you are Sara's reincarnation. And they are coming after you."

FOURTEEN

DANCING WITH DEATH

Days passed, and Navratri came. I had went shopping with my Aunt Tulsi. It was fun. I enjoyed a lot. Did I forget to mention that it was the only part of Navratri I enjoyed?

The music buzzed loudly till late night, you had to dance with insects going in your eyes and handing a thousand pounds outfit. And you had to do it over and over again, for nine days. And the height was that people actually enjoyed doing Garba. Most of the times, I would make an excuse and stay at home. But this time, there was Garba at my school, and I had promised my friends I would come. Don't ask me why I did that. I was being plain stupid.

My Aunt Krishna helped me get ready for Garba. I was looking very pretty, not that I cared. But for the first time, I craved for those godly looks. I thought of how Amara's face lightened up, like it was a luminous star. I wasn't jealous, but I couldn't imagine being so gorgeous. Having flawless hair, jewel like eyes, inhuman-strength. I part of me wanted that. But the other part, the more sensible one, shut it up. It was very immature of me to want that, of course it was.

My brother dropped me to my school. I quietly hopped out of his car and ran childishly to my friends clutching the sides of my skirt as to avoid tripping over it. Hours went by playing. I was surprised at the fact that I was having fun. A teacher asked me and some of my friends to accompany her to a classroom to help her get some boxes. As we did Garba, I felt sweat trickle down my throat. I used my hand to wipe it off, but that was when I realized that the necklace, given to me by Amara, was missing. I asked a teacher if I could go back to the classroom to find a very expensive piece of jewellery, and since she was too lost in a conversation with another teacher, she said yes without even considering my words.

I walked down the halls to the empty classroom. The lights were off, so I turned them on and found myself face-to-face with Stanford.

"You are following me, why?"

"Maybe because I want to kill you."

"Or maybe...?"

"Maybe I wanted to see my beloved dead wife." He laughed cruelly.

"I wanted to apologise, for my behaviour the other day. I didn't wish to put salt on your wounds."

"I am not wounded!"

"Yes, you are. You are hurt. Let me help you."

"Help me with what? I don't need your help. And I am not hurt." I had no idea why, but he had a knife in his hand. Maybe to scare me or to kill me.

"Well then, I won't be sorry for doing this if it won't hurt you." I put my hand on his hand which was carrying the knife and stabbed myself with all my force. It was a risk. I felt sharp pain in my stomach and I collapsed on the floor as he let go of the knife.

"Well, that was pretty stupid. You seriously thought I would care for you? I killed you once, or seven times if we are being precise. Most of them were when you were an infant. I have no mercy or love for you. The only reason you alive for so long, was because I wanted to see how much you believed in me. Well, now that this is all over, I can finally go back to San Francisco and resume my never-ending vacation," he walked over me and left the room, and there I lay, helpless, unable to shout and in unbearable pain. I closed my eyes; I knew it was coming. Thanks to my hunter hearing, I heard voices.

"Where is she?" Amara begged, her voice breaking.

"Why should I bother?"

"Dad, please. It's mom. You loved her for more than four centuries. You were with her. How can you be so cruel?"

"See, she has a fatal wound. She is going to die, again. By my hands. And I don't care, to be honest this needs celebration. The eighth assassination of Sara-" I head a slapping sound, and I knew what had happened. "Okay, that was a little over the top."

"Where is she?"

"It's the fifth classroom, walk up straight." I heard ascending footsteps. And in a matter of moments, I found my head in Amara's lap. She called an ambulance, and I could barely hear her speak motivational words to keep me awake. I blacked out as some people put me on the stretcher.

I woke up in a hospital ward. You would've thought by now I would be used to waking up in hospital wards. Turns out you can never get used to waking up to find a thousand needles in your body and yourself in a very ugly hospital gown. The smell of roses filled my nose, and I saw a beautiful vase filled with roses. There was a letter under it. I opened it and read.

Sarika,

Hey. I am sorry for what I did, but you must understand I only did it for Amara. I know roses don't cover it, nor does any apology, but know that I am at your side.

Love,

Stanford

I smiled to myself. I wasn't surprised. I was putting the paper back under the vase, when I heard a voice, "Well, that seems like a positive reaction,"

I got so scared that I yelped and turned to the follow the source of the voice. Stanford sat there as if he had been sitting there all along, which was so not the case. I threw a pillow at him.

"Just cause you are faster than normal humans, does not mean you have to show it off."

"Forgive me, madame," he sarcastically said, rolling his eyes. But then he got serious. "I am so sorry you are hurt."

"It's not your fault."

"You have no idea how much it is my fault. I was a coward, I should've fought. I shouldn't have just let you die." I didn't know what to say, so I just remained quiet. "You have the right to be mad."

"Well, I am not mad. How can you expect me to be mad about something I don't remember."

"I did threaten you at that café. And you are here because of me."

"You could've killed me earlier, it's not like you didn't have any chances to do that. Consider me being grateful for that."

"Grateful for not killing you? That way you should be grateful towards everyone on this planet for not killing you,"

"I wish I could say that it was funny." His hand went into his pocket and he pulled out a silver necklace. The one Amara had given me.

"You dropped it." I didn't know what to say or do. Whether to take it or tell him I was ready to fight. He made no moment, he neither offered it to me nor did he put it back. He looked at me expecting to make a decision, but when I looked away and got into a more comfortable sitting position, he spoke, "I would understand, if you wish to live a normal life. But I won't lie and say that I would like it. Sarika, you are too young, I know that, and this isn't fair, but it's today or tomorrow."

"I don't know what to do. I don't know if this is right for me or not. Help me? Please..." I knew that we weren't close, but I trusted him to make the right decision.

"One day, you'll have a perfect family, a life with someone you love. And if they attack at that time, not only you, but everyone around you will be in grave danger. Even now, they are in danger. But Amun, Zakara, and Baif, they don't know yet that you exist. I can lie to them saying that you died. But later, if they find out, not only your life, but Amara's and your family's life in danger too. I can't make the choice for you, but my advice is that you fight right now, and not wait for yourself to get older. Cause as much as you want it, you will never be able to become normal or live like a normal person. And I am so sorry for that, but I think you should embrace this life, for the sake of everyone around you. The decision is yours."

"I trust you. And I believe you. But aren't they like halfway across the world? How am I gonna fight them?"

"I will lure them here, one by one, and then *we* will fight them. But there is one obstacle in our plan."

"The weapon. It can kill you."

"And Amara," he added. "And I don't want anything to happen to *her*, Sara-I mean Sarika."

"Can't you just steal that weapon?"

"I wish it were that easy. I don't know where it is. They don't trust me *that* much."

"Stanford, wait, something just hit me. When I died, as Sara, the three of them were made immortal from my immortality. Does that mean that they are linked? Like, if we kill one of them, we kill the three of them?"

"There's a possibility, yes."

"And if they die, will *I* become immortal."

"Probably. I can just lure Baif here. He's the easiest to fool. Then you, or Amara can just kill him."

"Sounds like a plan. So, when do we do it?"

"After you get better. It can wait a couple weeks."

As if on cue, I suddenly felt pain on my wound and winced.

"Sarika?" Stanford asked worriedly. He quickly got up and walked up to me. "What's wrong? Is it your wound? Does it hurt? Do you want me to call the doctor?" I nodded frantically. The way he spoke, showed how much he cared for me. He put his hand on my cheek so tenderly, as if I would break into pieces if he applied the littlest bit of force. His hand made its way through my hair and held my head, which was getting heavier by the moment. "Doctor!" he called out so loud, that I was pretty sure that the whole hospital heard him yell. He gently lowered my head on the pillow and I blinked back tears of pain.

FIFTEEN

Dead Or To Be Dead?

A doctor entered my ward and told Stanford to leave the ward. He didn't argue, he just gave me one apprehensive look and left, closing the door of the ward behind him. The doctor dressed my wound back, gave me some painkillers and left, strictly ordering me to rest. I closed my eyes as I heard someone enter. The footsteps were highly muffled, which told me it was Stanford. But I didn't wish to talk to him at that moment. Cause I knew that I would be wary cause of the medications, and I didn't want him to see me as weak. So I just pretended to sleep. The room got awfully quiet after a while and I could feel eyes on me. I felt very uncomfortable but my discomfort was soon replaced by sleep. And more uncomfortable dreams.

I dreamt about the day I had died as Sara. How beautiful it was in the morning, and how dreadfully it ended. I and Stanford attended a fair, and our official status was unmarried, and we were on paper, strangers. It seemed crazy, but we were just having fun. We roamed around the world, most of the time as husband and wife, but sometimes, we tried crazy stuff, just for the fun of it. We were amongst the English, and so everything was very formal. And so was everyone, except, of course, us. Amara had come as my sister, cause I looked too young to have a twenty-six year old daughter. A Lord had asked Amara to dance with him and Stanford, being an overprotective father, had interfered and pulled Amara to dance with him instead. Back then, Amara was very cheerful, I could see it in the dream. I could see that she was getting bored, and so, I bribed the musicians to change to something more fun. To everyone's surprised, the waltz started getting faster. And so did everyone's dance. And then, after a little more bribery, the musicians started a very cheerful French song. Of course, some Lords and Ministers were highly offended, and it was a havoc. Everyone started dancing wildly as I took the violin. A power I had earned. I could charm worries and fake glamor away. And so, everyone danced openly. It was a wild evening. And during dinner, the three of us hid in the kitchen and threw food items at everyone. It was so childish of us all. And then we went back home. And he suddenly got upset. He hugged me and whispered, "I am so sorry, Sara." And then I felt shackles around my wrist and I pulled back, tears forming in my eyes, sensing his betrayal. I knew that with shackles around my wrist, there was no way I could fight him, but I still struggled. Amara was in the other room, and she heard the chains shackle. He was stronger than her, so he easily locked her back in her room, being careful that he didn't hurt her. He pulled me outside our house and to the woods nearby.

"What's going on, Stanford? Where are you taking me?" he ignored me and continued walking.

And then, I died. Amun, Baif and Zakara, killed me using the weapon, which was also a flower. Funny thing. They shoved a petal of that flower down my throat and used my immortality to link themselves. My throat burned terribly and then my stomach. I started coughing up blood. It all hurt so much. Even in the dream, I could feel the pain. And it was terrible.

I woke up with a jerk, still horrified from the dream. Someone was sitting on the edge of my bed, and I was still so scared that I hugged him without even looking at the face.

"Sarika, what's wrong?" It was my brother Reyansh. He patted my back as I cried.

"I had a dream. I died. And it hurt so much."

"You dreamt of the day you died as Sara?" Stanford asked. I hadn't noticed he was there. He sat on the chair, where he was sitting before. I nodded, letting go of my brother. "What did you see?" he asked, coming up to sit on the other side of my bed.

"I saw the three of them, Amun, Baif and Zakara. It was so painful, dying."

He looked at me with pity and pain. I could tell that he was upset and hurt. And I didn't want him to be. I hastily wiped my tears, not wanting to hurt him any further. "You don't have to act strong on my account," he assured gravely, looking at his feet. I muttered quietly, "I am sorry."

"You don't have anything to apologize for," he replied taking my hand and looking at me in the eye. "The fault was mine, not yours. So, don't blame yourself, okay? Now tell me, what exactly did you dream of?"

"I saw you and Amara dance. And the rest of the day. That night. When I died. How I died. I saw everything. And I felt everything. The pain. The agony. The hurt. I felt it all. And I felt life being stripped away. I could feel being emptied of everything. As the immortality wore off, it felt like I was being skinned alive."

♡♡♡

The day before I was to be discharged, I was allotted a new nurse. She seemed like a very nice lady. She had small stretched eyes and beautiful curly hair. She was very pretty and her voice was like music. She gave me the pills I had to take after lunch. I ate lunch alone, since Stanford had disappeared since the day I had dreamed about the say I had died as Sara.

Amara was nowhere to be seen and everyone else was just too busy with their work. After lunch, I took the medicines and went back to sleep, cause well, I had nothing better to do. I woke up with an ache in my chest. I wanted to puke. I got up and ran straight to the bathroom where I vomited. A nurse, the same new one, entered my ward as she heard me coughing loudly.

"It won't be that painful this time, you know." She said putting a hand on my back and offering me a glass of water.

"What are you talking about?" I asked taking a sip of water.

"Dying. It won't hurt that much." She spoke smiling.

"Who are you?"

"I am Zakara. And you are a threat, and threats need to be eliminated."

"What's happening to me?"

"You're dying. But worry not, you'll be just fine. You have a few hours to say your farewells." She turned around and left quietly. I didn't know what was happening. The water helped a little. I huddled up beneath a bundle of blankets.

"I met Zakara outside! What happened, Sarika?" asked Stanford in an anxious tone, entering the ward.

"She said I am dying. I think she poisoned me."

"Do you have Amara's number?"

"No, but my brothers might."

"Tell me your brother's number." I did. He called my brother who shared Amara's number with him. He quickly called Amara. "Hi Amara. It's Stanford." Awkwardness was clear in his voice. "Zakara poisoned Sarika. You need to come here. Now."

"Right, we are on the same team now. I'll be there." She said coldly and the line went off. Stanford sadly put down the phone but then smiled for my sake.

"Now, unless you want your daughter to murder me, I suggest you don't die on me." Amara was there in a matter of minutes. She didn't even look at Stanford and she quickly started taking my temperature and checking other symptoms.

"You know what I find strange here? That the only person apart from her family and me who knew who she was, was you. So, please tell me how the hell did Zakara find out about Sarika?"

"I was trying to lure Baif here. Instead I got the Poison Queen."

"Lure Baif?" she turned with disbelief to me and then to Stanford. "Should I even ask."

"We figured out that if we kill one of them, the three will die. So, well, we planned to lure Baif here."

"*We*? She doesn't even know how strong they are! Where were you, by the way?"

"On and about the city. Look, this is not my fault!"

"Is that what you are going to tell yourself when she dies?"

"Amara. It's poison. You are a healer. I know she won't die." Amara exhaled loudly.

"It's an old poison. I don't know how Zakara got her hands on it. The items used to prepare the antidote have ceased to exist. But, there is another way. I can suck the poison."

"No. You can't hurt yourself for me!"

"Believe me, the worst that can happen to me, is a common cold. So don't worry." She took my hand which started illuminating on her touch. My nausea started vanishing. I didn't feel so cold anymore. As soon as Amara took her hand away, I felt normal. She smiled at me, but that smile disappeared after a moment and she whispered agitated, "What are we gonna do now?"

"I am gonna kill Zakara for this!" I replied aggressively. Stanford and Amara both chuckled at that. "What?" I questioned, huffed.

"Nothing. You just look very cute when you are angry." Amara replied.

"I am not trying to look cute. I am serious and I am angry," they both laughed more at that, but then Amara said seriously,

"You're not going to kill Amara. I'll do that. We both have a little tiff to settle." She and Stanford exchanged a glance.

"Don't die." He said nodding. She left the ward and I asked Stanford,

"What tiff?"

"There was a boy Amara loved once. Zakara, in her attempts to poison Amara, poisoned him. Poor lad died horribly."

I looked away at the afternoon sun. I was tired. I was angry. But moreover, I was praying for Amara. That she be safe. My prayer weren't left unanswered. As dusk passed, she appeared. There was blood and dirt on her face, but her survival meant that she had won.

I was surprised how easily it had all ended, at least I thought it had. Apparently, I was still a problem. I didn't know if I was immortal or not, but at that moment I didn't care. I was discharged at evening and so, we all went out to celebrate. Me, my family, Stanford and Amara.

At night, Stanford and I were talking in my room, Amara was with my brothers, they had all gone out to enjoy, while my dad was out thanking gods for their help.

"I don't feel any different, you know. I don't think I am immortal."

"You aren't. It didn't work" He pulled out a knife. "This has to end. I don't want you to get into more trouble, Sara. You die this time, you'll finally get peace. It will be all over."

"No!" I protested.

"I am sorry, but this is the only way. You might wanna close your eyes."

"It'll hurt!" I complained as tears fell from my eyes.

"Just for a bit. Trust me." I closed my eyes. There was pain. A lot of it. And then, everything went blank. There was darkness everywhere. I couldn't see a thing, not even my own hands. I was scared to walk, afraid I would fall, but I started walking anyway. Suddenly, I was gripped from all sides by illuminating ropes and I felt very light, and then realized I was floating in the air. I felt pleasant. It was a wonderful feeling. I felt whole, complete, filled with strength and happiness. And suddenly, the ropes let go of me, and I fell but I never hit the floor. I kept falling for what felt like an eternity and then slowly zi zapped out of there, to a little less darker room. I opened my eyes, which I never remembered closing. My head was heavy, with all the sudden rush of memories that I had had. I got up and saw my wound, which had healed. I made my way out of my room to the hall. The house was dark but I could still see things.

"Who's there?" I heard Stanford call. I didn't reply, I kept walking to the source of voice. "Sarika?"

"No. Try again!" I replied in a playful tone.

"Sara!"

The End

Who-the Tale Of Mrs. Anonymous

1- The Dawn

The morning sun rose high in the sky as the clouds parted away and the chilly rainy night came to an end. Lyric took the coffee mug from beneath the cappuccino maker and pulled over the chair to the coffee table. She raised the trivet mat to obscure the sunlight coming from the glass window.

Thievery of the Purple Diamond of Mr. Francis! She read the tittle of the newspaper headline.

The term felt familiar to her. She turned around to her husband who was too filling his mug with cappuccino. "Cliff! Wasn't this jewel present at the party yesterday?"

Clifford, her husband sat down on her right. "Yeah, it was there!"

"*October second, When the party for the memorial of Lady Maragaret also known as Mrs. Frances at the Courtenay Mansion was going on, an expensive and ancient jewel was stolen. Lady Valarie, called the cops at the first sight of the empty glass of the jewel. However, she denied to give the permission to investigate during the party so the party comers could enjoy themselves. Resources say that the investigation would begin today without further ado.*"

She flipped through the pages of the newspaper to find that mostly whole of the newspaper was covered in the articles about the jewel, its thievery and Mr. Francis.

Token of Love stolen in the city known for love

"Love! Is that all Paris is known for?" she spoke angrily keeping down the newspaper. "Speaking of which, are you telling me that someone stole a jewel in the party that was *here?*"

"Yeah!"

"And you didn't even consider telling me?"

"Mom told me to keep it a secret! *What would people say if they found out that someone stole in this reputed house!*" he mimicked his mother.

"Exactly what they are saying right now!" she snapped.

"Well, she did tell the cops to keep it a secret!"

"It doesn't take long for a news as popular as this to leak!" she gaped as she heard some slow music coming from somewhere close.

"Your phone!" Cliff said handing her phone. "Mom told me to change the ringtone after last night's incident!" Lyric felt embarrassed at its memory. But was spared from remembering it again as the ringtone grew louder. It was Sir Patrick.

Of course! She thought.*He would want to know more about the thievery.*

She put the phone on speaker so that her husband could hear how bad it is to know nothing about something that has happened in your own house.

"Good Morning sir!" she recounted. It was what people expected her to say now.

"Doctor Bouvier! I heard about the thievery that has recently taken place at your house and couldn't resist to ask you if you wanted to take part in the medical investigation!" he suggested elaborately.

"It wasn't at my house; it was at my mother-in-law's house!" she corrected him imagining Lady Valarie's expression if she heard someone say it was her house. "But sure sir! I would be glad to be a part of it!" Lyric nervously replied and put down the phone. She scanned the newspaper again for some other news and stopped as she came across an article. "*Mrs. Anonymous unseen for now more than two years. The last person to see her in her disguise was Mr. Bakers from down the street of the Jewel Gallery. He is also the only known alive person to see her. 'She has blond hair and fair skin.' He informed. On the bases of his statement, the cops have changed the name of Mr. Anonymous to Mrs.*

Anonymous. Till now she has left no trace in any of her thefts and killings. She has been the smartest thief of all the time. The cops think she has been planning for something big." she read. "Only person *alive*......planning for something *big*...!" she repeated.

"How many girls you know have blonde hair and white skin?" Cliff scoffed.

"Huh! Never mind, I gotta go, Sir Patrick is counting on me to solve this mystery like always." She responded nonchalantaly. She hurriedly dressed up into some work clothes and left.

She was in her cabinet noting down the weather of the previous night when she heard a knock at her cabin door.

"Yes?"

The door opened as Mr. Enif Fawaris came into the cabinet. He had red hair and shallow violet eyes. "It's like we meet just yesterday!"

"Technically we did for the Wardley Murder case!" Lyric replied standing up from her desk and handing out the report she was finishing. "Fog level, visibility and everything!"

"Just like always! How do you always know what I am going to ask for!"

"Experience!"

"How long have you been here?"

"Two year!" she slowly replied.

"You really are a fast learner!" he exclaimed suspiciously.

"Actually, I worked as a cop myself for three years in New York."

"That's great!" he said, though not fully convinced. "At the crime scene at 1 PM sharp!"

"I'll be there!" she gazed at the mirror at the back of her cabinet door as Enif left closing the door behind him. She looked inside her own purple tourmaline eyes. Tying her beautiful brown hair, she sat back on her seat noting down some more facts that might help in solving the mystery. Hours passed faster than ever. It was the gratitude of her job that no one was calling her but she knew that the minute the hour hand would strike 8 there would be gazillions of calls from her formal relatives. There was only one call in the whole day and that was from her husband to confirm if she was fine or not and partly to ask her favourite colour.

"Why don't you join the cops again?" Mr. Enif said sophistically looking at all the Four-dimensional projection of the house with all the rooms and open spaces in it. "No wonder there were no robberies in New York Two years ago!" Lyric gave a small smile to this complement.

The investigation begun. There was no trace or sign. No footprints, no fingerprints, nothing. They investigation team was halfway through checking the glass of the jewel for fingerprints when Enif spoke, "We need to open this glass box. Call Lady Valarie!" he commanded his assistant cops.

Two junior cops rushed to call Lady Valarie. They later came back with an old pale lady with wrinkles on her face. Her hair was dyed dark black and her old suspicious eyes were moving from person to person. She was wearing a purple frilly gown with net gloves and heavy accessories. "What do you want?" she questioned shadily.

"We want you to open this glass box!" Enif said with high respect.

"Turn that way! *All of you!*" she barked.

Everybody turned their backs to the glass box as Lady Valarie approached to give the pin to the high security safe.

Lyric wondered why Lady Valarie was being so cautious towards a box that's empty.

"Here you go! But I don't think you have made the right choice in the forensic department! You should not select people who keep cry-baby songs as their ringtones!" Lady Valarie turned to Lyric. As she left, Enif asked, "What was it about?"

"Yesterday during the party John called me to inform me that the Wardley case was solved and the murderer was caught! Unfortunately, my ringtone was an emotional slow song and the volume was loud enough for everyone to hear!" Lyric replied, embarrassed.

"Don't worry Lady Valarie has always been like this! She called me a week ago to say that the jewel was missing. She opened the safe to find that it was one of her own tricks to trick the thief into believing that the glass box was empty. She is getting old, you know!"

"Yeah, you don't think it was Mrs. Anonymous, do you?"

"For a second I did think that!"

"Then-?"

"Sources say either she is dead or she has got rich enough to stop stealing!"

"What if she was planning for this big thing?"

"Sources have not reported a single unusual activity or a hooded black jacket person roaming around!"

"And what do you think?"

"I think we are going to solve a really big case!"

It seemed as though the news reporters were thinking the same thing. The whole newspaper was covered in articles about the previous robberies of Mrs. Anonymous. It was another day of failed investigation. No clue! Not a single one! The case was getting complexed by the moment when Lyric suggested to call the party comers for investigation. There were around twenty ladies invited. All of them belonging to a wealthy family.

"Do you have doubt on someone?" Enif asked Lady Valarie.

"All of them have Royal blood flowing through every vein in their body! None of them would do that! The last thing I want to do is accuse those ancient relatives of mine!" she deviously replied and left.

2-The Party

The huge mansion was decorated conventionally in a royal way. Everybody was busy chatting with each other. A group of ladies were laughing in a fake sense so loudly that it almost made Lyric drop her goblet filled with water. The sophisticated talk and formal dressing were already making her nervous when Lady Valarie called her to introduce her to others. She tried to walk as straight and normal as she could but was stumbling due to the heals, Lady Valarie made her wear. She hoped that Lady Valarie wouldn't realise that she had changed into some short and little fewer stumbling heels.

She's wearing peep toes heels, which matched the dress perfectly. To top it all off she's wearing a subtle necklace and an ornate bracelet. The dress left her shoulders uncovered, instead it supported around her neck and flew down into a tasteful square neckline. It's comfortably fit but by still looking elegant. Her arms had been covered to just below her elbows. The sleeves broadened towards the bottom and playfully accentuated her skin.

"This is Lyric Bouvier, my daughter-in-law, daughter of Mr. Lawrence Bouvier. Married my son six months ago. She belonged to a wealthy and royal family but their culture was quite different! She lived in Los Angles, that's why but she's

really intelligent and beautiful."

"Thanks M-Lady Valarie!" she changed her sentence as Lady Valarie looked at her in alarm.

"You are right Lady Valarie! She is an angel!" said a young lady with designs covering her face. It looked as though she had painted the make-up on her face. She was the only person who wasn't wearing those net gloves in her hands. The dress covered her shoulders halfway and flew down into an elegant draped neckline. It's a loose fit. Her arms had been covered to just above her wrists. The sleeves broadened towards the bottom, allowing for bracelets to be visible. The dress' waist was thin, but it's a loose fit. A cloth ribbon had been wrapped around her and has been tied on one side. Below the waist the dress widened and had multiple symmetric layers from top to bottom. The dress reached all the way down, almost covering her feet and was the same length all around. She's wearing ballerinas, which matched the dress perfectly. To beautify it all she's wearing a pearl necklace and a colourful stone bracelet.

"This Ms. Soliel Calistèe de la Roche! An artist! Her family was in debt seven years ago but her paintings saved the honour of the family."

"I believe that art is the creator of the world. Without art it would be impossible for the humans to imagine!" she said moving her fingers in a unique style.

"True!" replied a lady who unlike others was clutching a metal goblet with ancient designs carved in it.

"And this is Lady Esmerelda!"

"Hello!" Lyric said politely.

"You're as pretty as peach!" she exclaimed graciously looking at her clothes.

"Thank you?" Lyric replied smiling nervously, confused if it was a compliment or a sarcasm. "You want me to bring you a glass goblet?"

"Oh no, no, no...young'un. Glass doesn't amount a hill of beans does it?" she replied heartily. "Oh rats!" she cried suddenly and Lyric thought that were real rats so before thinking she cried- "Where?"

"Very funny-your daughter-in-law is!" Lady Esmerelda continued smiling in a good way as Lady Valarie patted Lyric on shoulder, laughing, trying to keep her silent. "I am sure she'll fit in soon! Don't worry Valarie, you ain't raisin' cain! Well, Valarie, I am surprised you have kept crawdads on menu! I thought you used to dislike them!"

"They are just for you Lady Esmerelda!" Lady Valarie replied. Lyric was surprised Lady Valarie was being called by her name. "Ah! And there goes Leigh for the speech! She is a historian!"

Lyric saw on the stage a blonde-haired girl holding the microphone in one hand and looking at the middle of the crowd. "We have all gathered here to celebrate a hundred and twenty years since Lord Francis gave Lady Margaret who is more commonly known as Lady Frances since that day when Lord Francis gave her the Purple Diamond!" Leigh said looking a little right to the glass box in which the jewel was kept, then back to the crowd. "Hope you enjoy this special treat by Lady-" she broke off as she heard some song playing.

"Oh...missed you for longer then you know! Come back..." It wasn't long till everyone tracked the source of music. It was coming from Lyric's purse. "My love..." Lyric opened the purse and started searching for her phone. She found it and muttered in a tiny voice- "Excuse me!"

She left for her room. Behind her, she heard Leigh start her speech again.

"Yes!" she picked up the phone.

"Lyric! It's me, John!"

"Yeah what's wrong?" Lyric replied hoarsely.

"We caught the murderer of Wardley!"

"Big deal! You called me just to say that?" Lyric continued speaking coarsely.

"Yeah why?"

"You know there is a party going on here and I am there! What was so urgent!"

"I am sorry if I disturbed you, your highness!" he remarked sarcastically.

"I am sorry!" Lyric sighed, realising her mistake. "It's just all these rules and everything is so rigid here! You can't even laugh your head off at a joke properly. Never mind! Tell Owen to check the files again so that we could close the case! I'll be in touch soon bye!"

She wasn't willing to face everyone again. The pressure was too much for her. So, she decided to make an excuse when someone asks her and stay there until somebody does. With tears on the edge of her eyes, she sat down on the extra comfortable bed. She looked at the newspaper kept on her pillow which she thought was by Cliff. She read the tittle- Mrs. Anonymous doesn't exists

Information leaked from inside the department. Mr. Anonymous, now known as Mrs. Anonymous, is a shady character, created from the imagination of one of the high positioned officers. 'No such man or woman exists! The character was created to hide the fact that many smart thieves are roaming around the world!' an inside person was overheard saying this to his friend.

However, Mr. Lawrence Bouvier still doubts that his daughter was kidnapped by Mrs. Anonymous for unknown reasons when Mrs. Anonymous stole a really expensive jewel from their house two years ago. A really expensive, Blue Pearl, one of its kind. He states that Lyric, his daughter, might have seen the face of Mrs. Anonymous and she would have either kidnapped or killed her.

Lyric's heart fell as she read those words said by her father. He missed her. He was there looking for her while she was here, attending a party in an ornate gown. How would he feel when he knows it? It's thought made her throat dry. What if Mrs. Anonymous had kidnapped her? Her father was half right! She had seen Mrs. Anonymous! But Mrs. Anonymous hasn't realized that she had seen her half face! Or had she? What if this was the big thing Mrs. Anonymous was planning for? To kill her!

3-Two Years Ago-The Theft at the Bouvier's

It was a deep dark night. With everything silent. Just one sound. The ticking of the clock. The Bouvier Manor was surrounded by high protection. Not even an ant could crawl in alive. Everyone was in their rooms. Everyone except Lyric. She liked night time strolls. She was walking at the edge of the lake, closely followed by a person. She had no idea that she was being followed. She was as surprised as anyone could be when she turned and saw someone standing behind her. She was so shocked that she fell in the lake. She wasn't a big fan of being in muddy water at the middle of night. Even if her father had told her a billion times that there was nothing in the lake, she was still afraid that the lake was filled with poisonous huge snakes. She yelled for help and the person following her gave a hand to her so that she could get up. For a second, she considered staying in the lake but the thought of being eaten by snake made her take the hand. She slowly got up to her feet at her hands touched the mud at the edge of the lake.

"Who are you?" she asked the person.

"Your personal bodyguard! Mr. Lawrence has asked me to stay close to you to protect you!" Lyric knew exactly why her

father had given these orders. Three precious stones were stolen in the previous month. Mr. Anonymous was getting more popular and the media had its full attention on Mr. Anonymous. The Blue Pearl in the centre of the manor was really precious. And her father was sure that it was the next victim of Mr. Anonymous. And something that happened a week ago made him more scared.

After the stealing the Rainbow Quartz, someone saw Mr. Anonymous's face without Mr. Anonymous realizing. He informed the police as soon as he got home as he was afraid to leave his house, in case Mr. Anonymous had realized. "I saw him!" he cried as soon as the police picked up the phone. "I saw Mr. Anonymous! I know how he looks!" The police asked for his address and came over. But when he didn't open the door, they had to break the door to find him lying on the floor. Dead. The news had spread like wild fire. No one wanted to leave their houses. There was a curfew for a day and people stopped attending galleries. Unique stone galleries in particular.

"Okay, I'll go to my room and grab a towel!" Lyric affirmed.

"Wait! I have a towel for you!"

"Why?"

"In case someone pushed you in the lake!" he replied opening a suit case behind him that Lyric hadn't noticed till that time. He handed her the towel but that was not what Lyric wanted. She wanted him to go away and leave her alone.

Pretending to shiver, she spoke in a broken voice- "I need to change into some warm clothes! I am going to my room!"

"Stop Miss! I have clothes for you!" he said handing her a pair of clothes.

"But I can't change here! I am going to my room!" she left, shuddering for real. The night was getting colder by the moment. As expected, she was still being followed by her guard. She opened the door to her room and turned to the guard.

"I'll be here ma'am! Outside your room! Call me if you need me!"

"Sure!" Lyric retorted closing the door. She looked at the glass window. She could use a rope and get inside the cellar using the emergency exit door. She ambled towards the open window and saw a rope dangling. She pulled it to check its strength. "Strong enough! Looks like sister has figured out this shortcut to reach the pearl. I thought she didn't have a brain! Hopefully, she won't post it on internet. Or else even Mr. Anonymous would find out. She carefully climbed down from the rope to the top of the cellar in which the pearl was kept. As she can closer to the roof, she noticed the top was cut in a square big enough for a human to slid down. She couldn't keep her foot on the top roof as the alarm would go off so she turned upside down and got a little down, to see who was inside. There was a person whose face wasn't visible though her shoulder length straight blonde hair were. There was ANONYMOUS written at the back of her jacket in a white. Lyric got back to her room, stupefied. She considered putting her foot down on the roof but chickened out when she noticed that Mr. Anonymous had a revolver. The only problem was that she had seen Mrs. Anonymous. It was a woman. And she had seen her. Without further thinking, she packed her bag. Before she realized, the alarm went off and she didn't wish to know how. So, she screamed and when the guard came, she distracted him and ran away.

The memory was still fresh in her mind. She was still worried if Mrs. Anonymous had seen her when someone kept their hand on her shoulder. She gasped and turned.

"Mrs. Esmerelda!" she sniffed.

"Bless your heart my child!" Mrs. Esmerelda. "You are just the spittin' image of me! I was once like you my child, not knowing what to say or not! But time taught me everything I

needed to know! And don't cry!" she added. "You can catch more flies with honey than vinegar! Now cut the lights off and come out! Valarie wouldn't want her daughter-in-law to be in her room during her great-great-great grandfather's party."

She came out of her room to the party back. Mrs. Judith was speaking something when suddenly Lady Valarie took out her phone and called someone and stepped out of the party hall towards and gave Lyric a stern look on her way out.

Mrs. Judith was standing close the jewel and the others were close to her. She was tapping her feet on the floor and fingers on her glass goblet. Everything was normal and everybody left one after the other and when the last person left, Lyric decided to sleep rather than wait for Clifford who was late to come back from his business office.

4-Lady Esmerelda's Confession

The memory was still fresh in her mind. She was still worried if Mrs Anonymous had seen her when someone kept their hand on her shoulder. She gasped and turned.

"Mrs Esmerelda!" she sniffed.

"Bless your heart, my child!" Mrs Esmerelda. "You are just the spittin' image of me! I was once like you my child, not knowing what to say or not! But time taught me everything I needed to know! And don't cry!" she added. "You can catch more flies with honey than vinegar! Now cut the lights off and come out! Valarie wouldn't want her daughter-in-law to be in her room during her great-great-great grandfather's party."

She came out of her room to the party back. Mrs Judith was speaking something when suddenly Lady Valarie took out her phone and called someone and stepped out of the party hall towards and gave Lyric a stern look on her way out.

Mrs Judith was standing close to the jewel and the others were close to her. She was tapping her feet on the floor and fingers on her glass goblet. Everything was normal and everybody left one after the other and when the last person left, Lyric decided to sleep rather than wait for Clifford who was late to come back from his business office.

***

“Do you doubt someone?” Enif asked Lyric.

“There is one person!” Lyric said suddenly. “Mrs Judith!”

The first person they investigated was Mrs Judith who, as said by Lyric was zooming around the jewel.

She was called to the interrogation room for investigation. She sat there nervous.

“My first question-Who are you?”

“The wife of the honourable Sir Raymond!” she said proudly twirling her hair and tapping inaudibly her feet on the floor.

“My second question-Why were you continuously walking around the Jewel box?”

“I wasn’t doing it on purpose! I was just talking with others when Valarie suddenly took out her phone and walked away in the middle of one of the favourite jokes! It was such a huge insult!” she continued jerking her legs.

“Go on...”

“It wasn’t the first time she had done something like that! She always thinks of herself above us all! Always prides on being a descendant of Lord Francis and Lady Frances!”

“So, you stole the jewel, the gift of Lord Francis to Lady Margaret, to prove that she was careless and did not deserve to be their descendant?”

"Me, no! How could you think such a thing! I-daughter of the great Lord Harold!" she stood up tapping her feet vigorously on the floor.

"Then why are you running away?"

"I am not-!" she started but Lyric interfered.

"She is not running away! She is telling the truth! She hasn't stolen it!"

"What makes you say that?"

"Look at that-!" Lyric pointed first at those jerking feet and then her hair clutched in her fist, her fingers twitching. "She has restless legs and fingers syndrome! She needs to keep both of them moving at least a little. So, she couldn't have possibly done that! Pricking the lock and all that!"

"Ok, someone else you doubt?" he said opening the door for Mrs Judith to leave.

"Maybe we should just call everyone one by one and investigate!" Lyric replied.

"I like that idea!" Enif replied. "Call Mrs Esmerilda!"

"I don't think she is guilty! She was with me during the time of thievery!" Lyric uttered nervously knowing that someone like Mrs Esmerilda cannot do something that could harm their respect.

"We don't actually know when the theft took place and interrogation is an important part of the investigation."

"Can we just at least go to get her ourselves, that would help!" Lyric urged hopefully.

Enif agreed. They all sat in the big car of the cops. Enif sat in the front beside the driver while Lyric sat in the back seat checking her phone. There was a message from Cliff. How are you and how is the investigation going? I will be late as I have to check on a business deal with an old client.

"Both are fine. At least for now. Enif reckons it's Mrs. Anonymous's one of the traceless thefts. If it is really her then I don't think it is going to be fine." She texted back.

There were at the huge residence in about fifteen minutes. It was even bigger ten Lady Valarie's mansion. That explained why Mrs. Esmerilda addressed Lady Valarie directly by name. They approached the huge house that was nearly the size of a castle. It was ancient but beautiful. There were guards at the entrance of the gates. Enif took out his identity card to show the guards but the guards, at the sight of Lyric, opened the metallically carved gates.

"The royal blood I suppose!" Enif muttered putting back his identity card. Lyric scoffed.

There was no doorbell near the door. Instead, there was a knocker. Lyric reached out a hand to knock. She expected Lady Esmerilda's maid to come and open the door but instead found herself face to face with Lady Esmerilda as the door opened.

"Oh! Lyric Bouvier isn't it!" Mrs Esmerilda cheered happily. Lyric peeped inside. Everything was made up of metal or few things were made of wood. Not a sight of glass. It felt strange to Lyric but she remembered what Lady Esmerilda said at the party "It doesn't amount a hill of beans!"

Lyric entered. Chandlers encircled the sitting area and lightened up the whole hall and engulfed everything in a flickering radiance. The illustrations of Paris in the sky on the bowed ceiling danced in the flickering light while stone effigies and carved images look down upon the oaken floor of this beautiful hall.

A magenta rug ran from the doorsteps down through the centre and split the hall into two paths leading out while ribbon banners with adorned ridges draped from the walls. Between each banner stood a large candlestick, a few of them lit and in turn illuminated the sculptures of heroes and leaders below them. Grand windows were covered by curtains coloured the same magenta as the banners. The curtains were adorned with burnished corners and decorating tips.

"Over yonder-" Lady Esmerilda gestured at the couch. Lyric sat at one side of the couch with Enif while Lady Esmerilda commanded her servants to fetch water. "So, what brings you here?"

"Um...we are here to ask you few questions about the thievery at Lady Valarie's mansion at the night when the party took place!"

"Heavens to Betsy! Thievery! At the party! What are you talkin' 'bout?"

"You don't know about the theft?"

"Of course, she does! She is trying to act innocent!" Enif sneered.

"Act innocent? What are ya talkin' 'bout?"

"Nothing! Enif I told you she cannot do something like this! We should go and interrogate the other guests!"

"Lyric! This is what I am talking about!" her voice suddenly clear. "You need to learn. If you are interrogating the other guests then you oughta interrogate me. It is important!"

"I get it!" Lyric nodded.

"Well, I need to confess then!"

"Confess what?" Lyric asked confused.

"That I did try to steal the jewel."

More Books By Me

VENTURES OF
GEM LAND-2
The Gorgon's
Curse
JANUSHI
RAICHURA

VENTURES OF
GEM LAND-3
The Alchemic
Presage
JANUSHI
RAICHURA

Enter Caption

9 798885 036634

Printed by Libri Plureos GmbH in Hamburg,
Germany